Will a freak accident destroy Callie and Morgan's happiness?

"The filter sounds different," Callie said. "Should we turn it off?" She took the dripping fern from Morgan, who walked over to the pool house and looked at the filter.

"There's a leak around the rim." He squatted down and examined the heavy two-foot diameter lid, running his finger around the seal. "If I tighten the bolt, that should take care of it."

That was one more thing Callie admired about Morgan—he didn't act like a big singing star or a corporate head. He was handy around the house. If he could fix something, he did.

She watched him locate the tool box on a low shelf and extract a pair of needle-nosed pliers. And then a horrific bang drowned out Callie's scream as she watched the lid blow off the filter and crash into Morgan's face, knocking him to the ground.

VEDA BOYD JONES writes romances "that confirm my own values." Jones lives with her husband, an architect, and three sons in the Ozarks of Missouri.

Books by Veda Boyd Jones

HEARTSONG PRESENTS
HP21—Gentle Persuasion
HP34—Under a Texas Sky
HP46—The Governor's Daughter
HP78—A Sign of Love
HP110—Callie's Mountain

Callie's Challenge

Veda Boyd Jones

Heartsong Presents

Dedication
To my in-laws, Merle and Marietta Jones,
for their encouragement and for their fine son.

Acknowledgment
Thanks to Joan Banks, Dian Doody, Bonnie Hinman,
Ellen Gray Massey, and Joan Schenk for their advice
on this book. Special thanks to my sister Elaine Jones
who survived this swimming pool accident. And of
course, thanks to Jimmie, Landon, Morgan, and
Marshall for their patience while I write.

A note from the Author:
I love to hear from my readers! You may write to me at the
following address: **Veda Boyd Jones**
Author Relations
P.O. Box 719
Uhrichsville, OH 44683

ISBN 1-55748-806-1

CALLIE'S CHALLENGE

Cover illustration by Gary Maria.

PRINTED IN THE U.S.A.

one

Callie Rutherford sang as she walked around the swimming pool absently checking the arrangements of plants. A clump of tall potted ferns waved their branches in the warm Atlanta breeze. In one corner a tiered plant stand held a blaze of colored azaleas. Tables, some with umbrellas, and chairs dotted the tiled deck.

"You sure sound happy," Wilda said, "singing in that sweet voice."

"I am happy," Callie told her housekeeper. As much as she wanted to confide her secret, she kept it to herself. Her appointment was in three days, and she'd say nothing until she was sure. She forced her thoughts back to the party and moved an artillery-leafed fern.

"Is that too close to the water?" Wilda asked.

"I think it's all right. Now what's left on our list?"

The party wasn't until tomorrow afternoon, but Callie wanted as much done ahead of time as possible.

"Caterers will set up tomorrow at eleven," Wilda answered. "I could have handled it, you know."

"I know," Callie agreed. "You're the best cook around, but I want you free to supervise changing rooms and such for the guests. I don't know how many will opt to swim, but we should be prepared. I want everything perfect."

This was Callie's first party since she and Morgan had married six months earlier. Although normally they would spend the May weekend in their mountain home in North Carolina, a couple hours' drive away, this weekend would

5

find them entertaining the board of directors of the
Rutherford Group.

No stuffy meeting for this group. Morgan had jumped at
Callie's suggestion of a family affair. Parents could bring
their children, and the older members of the board could
bring their grandchildren.

"I'm home," called a deep voice from inside the house.

"Out here," Callie called and watched her husband walk
through the french doors that opened from the house.

Every time she saw Morgan P. Rutherford III, or Trey
as his country music fans called him, her heart raced. God
had smiled on her and given her the love of the kindest,
handsomest, most talented man she'd ever know. A six-
time Grammy winner, he was also an astute businessman,
effectively combining his singing career with managing his
family's business empire.

Last week they had been in Nashville for the Academy
of Country Music Awards. Callie had stood in awe of some
of the music industry's brightest stars until she realized
they were all normal people; they just had high public pro-
files. Their success depended on the public liking their
music and their public image.

Trey had won several awards, including Entertainer of
the Year. In his acceptance speech, he attributed his success to God and his new wife, Callie.

The best music video winner even featured Callie. Since
Trey's manager Harry Caywood had insisted on filming
the benefit concert Trey had performed for Callie's small
country church, and since Trey had sung a special song
for Callie and proposed in front of thousands, the song
was a natural for a video—a touching one that fans adored

But that was last week. This week Trey had taken a back
seat to Morgan P. Rutherford III, business executive who

ran the Rutherford Group, an enterprise that owned six subsidiaries, from a theater to a small airline. Callie was proud that he could balance two such contrasting careers, but in her mind he was neither singer nor businessman. He was the man who loved her—the strong-principled Christian man to whom she'd given her heart.

Now Morgan strode outside by the pool and stretched his arms to Callie, who hugged him and lifted her face for his kiss. Even the little pecks he gave her when Wilda was around turned her inside out.

"Looking good," he said, as he glanced around the pool area. "Anything I can do to help?"

"I think we've got it under control," Wilda answered as she straightened some cushions on a chaise lounge. "We'll keep that filter running a little longer."

Arm in arm, Morgan and Callie strolled back into the house. "Talk at the office is of my clever wife who wants the board to know the executives on a casual basis."

"Good to know, but we'll withhold judgment until tomorrow," Callie said with a laugh, but she was pleased that Morgan's administrative heads were anticipating the pool party. The actual board meeting would be held a week later, an all-day Saturday affair.

After a leisurely dinner, Callie read over her party list and checked off a couple more items. "Want to walk?" she asked Morgan then. Many evenings they walked over their four-acre grounds for exercise.

They crossed through the kitchen to exit the back door. "Are you still here, Wilda?" Callie asked the housekeeper, who was wiping off the counter. "I thought you'd be getting ready for your date. She's going to the movies with Ralph," Callie explained to Morgan.

Wilda was in her early fifties and in the prime of her life, she repeatedly told Callie, who had to agree. Wilda had been widowed at an early age, had no children, had worked for Morgan for four years, and had been seeing Ralph a year longer than that.

"I'll change as soon as I turn off that filter," Wilda said as she hung up the dishcloth.

"Go on," Morgan said. "We'll turn it off on our way back in. By the way, I'm thinking of asking Ralph his intentions. This romance has been going on plenty long. Good thing it didn't take Callie that long to decide to marry me."

"You'll do no such thing," Wilda said with the familiarity of someone long accustomed to Morgan's teasing. She wagged a finger at him, but gave him a grin before leaving the kitchen.

Morgan and Callie, keeping a brisk pace, walked the perimeter of their land. Callie loved the well-groomed lawn with its neatly trimmed shrubbery. At first she'd found the high brick fence smothering, after the views from their mountain home outside of Highridge, North Carolina. But she'd quickly learned that even in this ritzy part of town, Morgan could easily be swamped by fans if he ventured into the neighborhood for an evening walk.

Being in the public eye had its drawbacks. They couldn't go out in public without causing a stir. Since that spontaneous proposal to her in front of a concert audience, Callie's and Trey's pictures had been splashed all over the tabloids. They had kept the actual wedding date a secret. The press had expected a Sunday afternoon wedding as the announcements had said. However, Morgan and Callie had called the guests at five o'clock on Friday and told them the wedding would be seven hours later at midnight. It had been a beautiful candlelight ceremony in the recently restored country church where Callie and her grandmother were members, and no reporters were around.

That reporters left Morgan alone at the Rutherford Group spoke of how completely he separated his two careers. Still, Callie was always aware that her moves were grist for public consumption, and the high walls around their grounds were a constant reminder.

"Shall we head back for the pool?" Callie asked. "Feels like we could have a shower." They had already walked the perimeter several times, and the evening breeze had turned into strong gusts.

"I'm ready to call it a night. We have a big day tomorrow. Don't worry. Even if it rains tonight, we'll have a good day for the picnic."

"Race you," Callie called over her shoulder as she sprinted toward the pool area.

Morgan caught her in no time, his longer stride on his side.

"Oh, no," Callie moaned, not because of losing the race, but because the wind had blown a fern basket into the pool, clouding the water with dirt and fine leaves. "I guess Wilda was right. I shouldn't have put that fern so close to the pool."

Morgan grabbed a net and fished the plant and basket out of the water, leaving some debris behind. "The filter sounds different," Callie said. "Should we turn it off?" She took the dripping fern from Morgan, who walked over to the pool house and looked at the filter.

"There's a leak around the rim." He squatted down and examined the heavy, two-foot-wide lid, running his finger around the seal. "If I tighten the bolt, that should take care of it."

That was one more thing Callie admired about Morgan—he didn't act like a big singing star or a corporate head. He was handy around the house. If he could fix something, he did.

She watched him locate the toolbox on a low shelf and extract a pair of needle-nosed pliers. And then a horrific bang drowned out Callie's scream as she watched the lid blow off the filter and crash into Morgan's face, knocking him to the ground.

Skin hung from his chin, exposing his jawbone. Blood shot from his flattened nose. "Morgan!" Callie screamed again. She knelt at his side and gasped at the widening circle of blood around his head. No, she couldn't lose Morgan now that they'd found such happiness.

What to do? What to do? She turned off the filter, which stopped the gushing water that soaked him, and then jumped up and ran for the house. Milliseconds later, she returned, shouting into a portable phone and dragging a tablecloth.

"Morgan Rutherford," she told the 911 operator. "Trey. It's Trey." She wasn't above using his fame to get the ambulance here and fast. She gave the address while holding the tablecloth to Morgan's nose, applying pressure to stop the bleeding. A wound in his neck bled, too, but it wasn't gushing like his flattened nose.

"I'm okay," Morgan croaked in a voice that wasn't his own. "I'm okay."

"I've got to unlock the gate." Callie tried to keep her voice calm, now that her initial panic was over. She guided Morgan's hand over the tablecloth. "Push down as much as you can stand. I'll be right back."

She carried the phone with her and dashed back into the house. There were several switches to the gate at the main entrance. She flipped the one in the kitchen while explaining to the operator what she knew of Morgan's injuries.

"Stay on the line until the ambulance gets there."

"I will," she said and ran back to Morgan. The puddle of blood was getting larger. His head, resting on one outstretched arm, was exactly as he had fallen. What she could see of his face was ghostly white against the red-stained tablecloth he still held to his nose.

God, please help him, she prayed silently. *Please, please don't take my Morgan.*

"They're on their way," she comforted him. She took over applying pressure and listened for the wail of sirens.

"I'm okay," Morgan croaked again.

"Yes. You're going to be fine," Callie said. She wanted to hug him to her, but she dared not move him.

After what seemed like hours, but must have been only a few minutes, she heard the scream of the ambulance.

"I hear them," she said into the phone. "Tell them to come around the house on the south side. There's a walkway."

Moments later a team of emergency personnel raced around the house, carrying a stretcher and a medical bag. Callie stepped back while two men hooked Morgan to an IV, applied a pressure pack to his face, and checked for broken bones.

On the count of three they lifted him onto the stretcher, with his head still resting on that outstretched arm. Callie followed them to the ambulance. Once Morgan was loaded, she climbed in beside him.

"Mrs. Trey, you can't ride with us. You'll have to follow in a car."

"No. I'm going with him, but I'll stay out of the way." She plastered herself to the side of the ambulance. The steel look in her eyes must have convinced the attendant that she wasn't budging.

"No time to argue. Let's go," he called to the driver, who

turned on the lights and siren as soon as the ambulance left the long driveway. Callie kept her eyes on Morgan's face as they careened around corners and raced through traffic lights. The technician talked to the emergency room via a speaker phone, giving Morgan's vital signs until they arrived at the hospital.

Callie waited until Morgan was unloaded before hopping out of the ambulance. She ran behind the stretcher and into the curtained cubicle with him.

The doctor pulled away the pressure bandage and Callie gasped. Morgan's face had puffed up, the swelling leaving a fold of skin that completely hid one eye. The other eye was a slit that looked straight at her.

"Okay," he said, or at least that's the guttural sound she thought he made over his raspy breathing.

"I know," Callie replied, holding back tears.

A receptionist came in with a form for Morgan to sign. "Can I sign that?" Callie asked.

"If he can sign, he should," she said.

Morgan's right arm still supported his head, but he moved the fingers of his right hand, motioning for the pen. Although Callie knew he couldn't see the paper above his head, he scrawled his name.

"We've got to stop the bleeding," the doctor said. "We'll stitch it, stabilize him, then operate."

Under protest, Callie was ushered out the door and into the lobby to wait. She used the time to call Morgan's mother from the receptionist's desk and told her what little she knew about Morgan's injuries.

"I'm on my way," Dorothy Rutherford said in a strained voice. The fear in her mother-in-law's voice echoed that in Callie's heart. She stumbled across the waiting room, collapsed in a chair, and cried.

"Oh, God, please help him," she whispered. "He's such a good man, and I love him so."

She took a deep breath and looked up when the receptionist called her Mrs. Trey.

"Could you fill out some forms, please."

"It's actually Mrs. Rutherford. Trey's his singing name," Callie said and sniffed. "What do you need?"

She took the clipboard and filled out all she could, then returned it. "I don't know our insurance number. I didn't grab my purse. Could I use your phone again?" She glanced at her watch. Nine o'clock. Would Wilda still be at the movies?

She looked up the theater number and had Wilda paged. After a couple of minutes, the housekeeper answered. She assured Callie she'd lock up the house and immediately bring the forgotten purse to the hospital.

Callie sat down again, then jumped back up and walked to the drinking fountain. She peeked through the glass in the swinging door that hid the emergency room cubicles from her view. Nothing. What were they doing in there? She paced to the front door and back. How long did it take to sew him up temporarily? And what would an operation mean? She took a deep breath and forced herself to sit down. She prayed again and again, then jumped up when she heard the swinging door open.

"We're taking him up to ICU," the doctor said. "The bleeding's under control, but it's not stopped completely. He's lost a third of his blood. I don't want to give him a transfusion if we don't have to, but we can't operate until his blood pressure is stable."

"What are you operating for?" Callie asked.

"We'll set his nose for one thing. I can't be sure until we get X-rays, but I think his jaws are broken at the hinges.

His palate doesn't look good. We'll probably have to put in a trachea tube for a few days, so he won't be able to speak. I don't know the extent of the damage from the blunt wound to his neck, although we're watching the swelling of his larynx. And we need a plastic surgeon to work on his chin. You can see him as soon as they get him settled in ICU. Don't upset him. He doesn't look like Trey. But he's conscious."

Callie nodded, then listened while the receptionist directed her to the intensive care unit. She took the elevator up and was whisked inside Morgan's room as soon as she identified herself to the nurse at the desk.

Morgan lay in the bed, holding a plastic suction tube in his mouth. "Oooo-kaaaa," he muttered through huge lips that stretched across his battered and discolored face.

"I know." Callie leaned over, brushed the hair off his forehead, and kissed him on a clean spot. His nose was flat. The multicolored bruises, which covered most of his bloated face, were darker under his slit of an eye. Dried blood covered his neck. Each time he took the suction tube out of his mouth to grab a raspy breath, he dripped blood on himself.

This person bore no resemblance to the dark-haired, blue-eyed, handsome man she'd married, except for the intelligent look in the one eye that stared at her.

"Here's your brother," a nurse said.

Callie glanced over toward the door and unconsciously moved in front of Morgan to block the view. Neither she nor Morgan had a brother.

A camera clicked.

"Get him out of here. He's a reporter," Callie ordered. She wasn't about to move or the man would see Morgan. The camera clicked twice more before the nurse ushered the reporter out.

"Sorry, Morgan," she said. "I'll speak to the nurses. I'll be right back."

Callie stormed out to the desk, where Morgan's mother now stood.

"You won't let her in, but you let in a reporter?" Callie said in a shrill voice. "A reporter with a camera!"

Dorothy Rutherford hugged Callie. "Calm down, honey. He's gone. Let's dwell on Morgan. How is he?"

"He'll be all right." She repeated all the doctor had told her. "You can talk to him, but he only grunts back. And you must be prepared because you won't recognize him. He looks . . . ," she searched for a word, "inhuman."

two

Before seven o'clock the next morning, Callie and Dorothy had been joined in the surgery waiting room by Morgan's sister, Victoria, and her husband, Adam; members of Morgan's band; Charlie Lockhard, Morgan's right-hand man; and several executives from the Rutherford Group. Wilda was on her way to North Carolina to get Callie's grandmother. Harry, Morgan's agent, had been at the hospital all night and had gone home for a shower.

Morgan had been in X-ray at six and was now in the operating room.

During the long night, Morgan had demanded a mirror. Dorothy had quickly handed him her compact mirror, so Morgan could examine only a small portion of his face at a time.

"The doctors are going to fix you up as good as new," Callie told him. And she believed it. She had talked with the plastic surgeon, who had assured her that he had seen worse facial injuries, and they had come out fine.

Callie had repeated the story over and over, from the horrific bang of the filter top blowing off to the moment Morgan had been taken downstairs, and she had drunk cup after cup of coffee.

"We've got trouble," Harry announced when he returned around eight. He waved a newspaper in his hand. "It hit the AP wire. That reporter knows the business." He handed the paper to Callie.

On the front page was a color picture of her blocking

16

most of Morgan's face. The side without a visible eye could be seen, but most people wouldn't be able to tell it was his face.

"SINGER INJURED IN FREAK ACCIDENT," the headline screamed.

Callie skimmed the article, which had exaggerated the facts, of course. An unidentified hospital worker had been quoted as saying Trey had no face.

"This is in every newspaper across the country this morning. No telling what the tabloids will run," Harry said.

"Should you release a statement after we know the extent of his injuries?" Callie asked. The last thing she wanted to think about was publicity, but she knew her husband's fans would want to know.

"I've already talked to a hospital administrator who will do it," Harry said. "We're setting up a press room."

Of course, she should have known Harry was on top of the situation. He was the best manager in the business. She'd heard Morgan say that often enough.

Morgan's minister arrived, followed by several members of the small congregation. Callie had found that his church home in Atlanta reminded her of the one she'd left in the mountains. Again, Morgan's public image led him to find a small church where he could know the few members and be accepted as another Christian there to worship instead of as a celebrity.

By nine o'clock, flowers started arriving, but there was still no word from the operating room.

Callie sat as long as she could, then paced around the large waiting room, speaking in polite tones to Morgan's friends, Victoria's friends, and Dorothy's friends, who now numbered at least thirty, standing in clumps or sitting in small groups, all waiting to hear word about Morgan. Callie walked over to the windows and stared out. She had been in Atlanta six months, but during that time she hadn't made any close friends of her own. For the first time since marrying Morgan she felt lonely and longed for the mountains and familiar faces.

Dorothy came over and held her hand. "How are you doing?"

"I'm all right," Callie said, although her nerves were stretched to the breaking point. She looked into Dorothy's eyes and saw the iron strength that Morgan had told her about. When his father had died, his mother had held the family together. Now she remained calm in the face of fear, while a tight fist squeezed Callie's heart.

"Shouldn't be much longer," Dorothy said. "Another hour, maybe. It's already ten o'clock."

Callie nodded, not trusting her voice. She watched hospital pink ladies carry in more flowers. Every end table was covered, and they were placing plants on the floor.

"I think I'll make a list of flowers," Dorothy said, digging in her purse for a pen and paper. Callie knew Dorothy was as wound up as she felt and needed something to do to pass the last few waiting minutes.

While Dorothy made her list, Callie escaped down the hall and found the hospital chapel. A couple in their forties sat at the back of the tiny room, the woman in tears. Although she had come there for solace herself, Callie stopped by their pew.

"Can I do anything to help?"

The woman shook her head, obviously unable to speak.

"Our son's been in a wreck," the man said. "He's in the operating room now."

"Jeff's only seventeen," his wife choked out.

"I'm sure the doctors are doing what they can," Callie

said. "He's in God's hands now."

The woman nodded, and Callie took a seat on the front pew to give the couple some privacy.

"Dear God," she whispered. "Please be with Morgan. He's such a strong man, but he's weak now. And please be with their son Jeff." She wiped a stray tear, refusing to give in to the emotions within her, and sat quietly for a while. She turned when she heard movement at the back of the room.

"Grandma," she said on a breath of relief and flew into the old woman's arms, the tears she'd held back flowing freely. Grandma had raised her from the day she was born, and since Grandpa's death years ago, Grandma had been both mother and father to Callie.

"I knew you'd be here, Callie Sue. Now, now, you dry those tears. God will take care of Morgan." Grandma reached into a deep pocket of her dress and handed Callie a handkerchief.

Callie stayed in the security of Grandma's arms until the storm had passed. "I guess we need to get back to the others," Callie said. "The doctor should be in soon."

Before they left the chapel, Callie spoke again with Jeff's parents, then she and Grandma walked slowly back to the waiting room. Callie was unprepared for the standing-room-only crowd.

Harry made his way to her side. "We've asked the hospital to keep others downstairs unless they're cleared by Charlie or me. No reporters are allowed up here. They're keeping them in another room. We've got major network cameras now. If this wasn't such a tragic event, I'd be thrilled with the coverage."

Morgan's sister squeezed through the crowd. "News has spread fast. Morgan's on every prayer chain in Atlanta and every other town in America. Don't you worry; he'll be fine." Victoria's eyes shone with unshed tears, but she smiled at Callie.

A moment later the doctor stepped off the elevator. The crowd quieted. Callie and Grandma walked over by Dorothy and waited for the news.

"He's fine," the doctor said first, and Callie could breathe again. "As we suspected, both his jaws are broken. He's wired shut and will be for six weeks. He has a new nose. His palate was shattered, and we're surprised he didn't lose more than two teeth with the force that had to have hit him to do this much damage to the roof of his mouth. He's breathing through a trachea tube now, so he won't be able to speak for a few days."

"Will he sing again?" asked someone from the crowd.

"I don't know," the doctor said and the group gasped. "A blunt trauma to his neck has caused the avulsion of a vocal chord. Time will tell what happens there. With more plastic surgery, we should be able to make the scars on his face less noticeable." He patted Callie on the arm. "He's in recovery now, but he'll be taken to ICU in about half an hour. Someone will come for you when you can see him."

The next half hour dragged by until Callie and Dorothy were ushered behind the closed doors of the intensive care unit. Morgan lay in the first cubicle with his eyes closed, drifting in and out of a deep sleep. His face was bandaged, but the swelling around his eyes was down, and he looked human again.

"Morgan." Dorothy held his hand, and for the first time silent tears flowed down her cheeks as she looked at her bruised son. Callie understood the relief that caused her tears.

"He looks so good," Callie said and meant it.

Dorothy gave a shaky laugh. "Who would have thought that this looks good? But you're right. He looks much better."

Morgan fluttered his eyelids, then opened them a second.

"I'm right here, honey. You're going to be fine," Callie said.

He nodded, a brief movement, and a sighlike sound escaped the trachea tube, as if he were reassured by her words.

Morgan's nurse moved in to take vital signs, so Callie and Dorothy stepped back into the ICU waiting room. Jeff's parents stood outside the door.

"How's your son?" Callie asked.

"The next twenty-four hours will tell," said Jeff's father. "He survived surgery."

"Have you seen him?"

"Not yet." He pointed to a sign behind Callie. Visiting hours in ICU were for five minutes every four hours. "They'll let us in at noon."

Callie stared at the sign. She had gone in and out of ICU all night, and so had Dorothy and Victoria. Why, even the reporter who claimed to be her brother had been admitted. Why couldn't this badly injured boy's parents see him? If she had reassured Morgan in some way, and she felt she had merely by her presence, then wouldn't parents have a remarkable effect on a seventeen-year-old boy?

"Your last name is?" Callie asked.

"Richardson, Ken and Marie Richardson."

"Callie Rutherford. I'll be right back." Callie twirled and opened the swinging door. A nurse sat at a desk in front of an aisle with five glass-fronted rooms on each side. Morgan was in the first room, but looking down the hall, Callie saw several empty rooms. In each room that held a patient, a nurse sat on a stool monitoring bleeps on complicated equipment.

"You can go back to him," the nurse at the desk said.

"Thank you, but why? When Jeff Richardson's parents are kept outside?"

"Now, we can't let everyone in here. They'd get in the way of treatment," the nurse explained.

"Then why am I allowed? It's not noon yet."

"Last night Trey told the doctor he wanted you in here."

But Morgan could barely talk last night. Although Callie had realized the rich and famous were treated differently, she naively hadn't expected that special treatment to spill into the medical world.

"So if Jeff said he wanted his parents—"

"He's unconscious right now," the nurse interrupted.

"But we don't know what unconscious people actually hear, do we?"

The nurse fiddled with some papers on her desk. "We're not sure," she admitted.

"What if Trey wants Jeff's parents with him?"

"Don't make this difficult, Mrs. Trey."

"Difficult? That boy could be dying. What if he were your son?"

The nurse actually blanched. "We try not to think in those terms," she said tersely.

Callie stared at her, speechless.

"Okay, I'll let them in," the nurse said as she rose from her chair. "But I'm holding you responsible. The head nurse will be back in a few minutes. If I get in trouble . . . ."

"I'll take the blame," Callie said and followed her into the ICU waiting room. Jeff's parents were led inside, and Callie and Dorothy trailed back to Morgan's room.

Callie watched Jeff's parents. His mother didn't cry now,

but stood tall and held her son's hand. Soft crooning noises could be heard. "You're fine, son. Don't worry. Dad and I are here."

The comforting sounds were much like she had murmured to Morgan during the night, and she had seen him visibly relax at the sound of her voice. Callie knew she had done the right thing in interfering with hospital policy.

Morgan still slept, so Callie and Dorothy returned to the surgery waiting room.

"He's much better," Callie told the crowd. "He'll be moved to his own room tomorrow."

"Did he talk to you?" someone asked.

"He can't talk. Remember the tube? But I'll bet he'll be writing notes in a few hours," Callie said.

And he was. By late afternoon, Morgan was talking with his own brand of sign language and scribbling notes on a pad that Callie got at the hospital gift shop.

The crowd had dispersed, although Victoria, Grandma, Harry, and Dorothy remained. Charlie had asked that Rutherford Group executives go home.

"Morgan's orders," he said after making a quick trip into ICU. He held up a scrap of paper to prove his words. "Sorry about the picnic. We'll do it soon," he read.

ᔥ

By that evening, Morgan was moved to his own room with a private duty nurse. Normally a patient with his injuries would have been kept in ICU, but there was too much traffic in and out, the head nurse had said. Callie knew the move was a direct result of her interfering with Jeff's parents, but since she could afford the private duty nurse, she much preferred that Morgan be in a cheerful room than in the trauma atmosphere of ICU.

She told Morgan about Jeff. After their first visit to their son, Ken and Marie Richardson had to wait until the regular visiting time to see him again, so Callie showed up in the waiting room right after each visiting session to get an update on Jeff's condition. Although a fifteen-year age difference separated them, Callie and Marie became fast friends, bonding with the weight of their traumatic experiences.

By bedtime, Callie was exhausted but refused to go home for longer than the time she needed to take a shower and change her clothes.

"You're paying the nurse to stay with him," Dorothy told her.

"I know, but I can't sleep at home. I'll do better with Morgan." Just because Morgan was out of ICU didn't mean he was out of the woods. Even the slightest possibility of hemorrhage meant she wasn't going to leave him.

She spent the night in a reclining chair and got up each time Morgan stirred. He wrote on the pad that he didn't want to take the pain medicine because it clouded his thinking and made him feel out of control. But Callie and the nurse convinced him that he'd get stronger quicker if he could sleep.

With morning came the arrival of more flowers. As soon as new ones were delivered and added to Dorothy's list, Callie set them outside the door for delivery to other wings in the hospital. She had kept about twenty arrangements to brighten Morgan's room, but there was no room for the other three hundred.

"Your fans love you," Callie told him. "And so do the florists in town." He smiled. It was just a millimeter raise of his swollen lips, but Callie knew it was a smile, and it warmed her heart.

"It's a miracle," Marie Richardson cried to Callie after

the noon ICU visit. "The doctor says Jeff's improving much faster than expected. He's off the ventilator and breathing on his own."

"It's the power of prayer," Grandma said when Callie announced it to the group that had gathered in Morgan's room.

Morgan was awake again and motioned with his hand for his paper and pen.

"I want to meet Jeff," he wrote.

"We'll arrange it when he's out of ICU," Callie said.

The doctor left orders for Morgan to walk. He would need time to regain his strength, especially since he had lost so much blood, but walking would begin the process of returning his body to normal. Before Morgan was allowed outside his room, Harry sealed off the corridor, closing doors to other rooms and stationing guards at the ends of the halls. He made sure there would be no photos of Trey in the morning papers, although updates of his condition were given on the nightly news.

Callie walked on one side of Morgan with his arm resting on hers for stability. Victoria walked on the other side and pushed the IV pole.

For two days that pattern continued, and Callie slept at home while a nurse stayed with Morgan. The morning the packing was removed from Morgan's nose, the doctor announced he'd take out the trachea tube the following day.

Callie saw the fear in Morgan's eyes even though the doctor assured him he'd be able to breathe when he took the tube out. Several times that day Callie watched Morgan cover the tube with his finger and try to breathe through his nose. Each time, he'd uncover the tube and make an awful gasping sound.

"I'm staying tonight," she told him about dusk that

evening.

He didn't protest but nodded in agreement.

"I have only a few more hours before you'll be able to speak, and I want to take advantage of it. For once you have to listen to me—you can't talk back." She winked at him.

The color of his bruises had changed daily, some to a deep red and others a mustard yellow, but although Morgan looked better, Harry was adamant in his stand on crowd control. After the reporter had managed admittance to ICU, Harry had set up a security system the FBI would admire. Besides controlling the group that had waited in the surgery waiting room, Harry kept a plainclothes guard at the door to Morgan's room, restricting visitors. Pink ladies left their flowers at the door. Only Morgan's privately hired nurses were allowed in.

Morgan still hadn't met Jeff. Harry felt a visit outside his wing, which was sealed before Morgan took his exercise walks, could cause problems. They'd arrange a meeting later.

Morgan didn't argue. He'd seen himself in the bathroom mirror, and he didn't want publicity now.

"I look bad," he wrote.

"I've seen you look better," Callie said. "And you will again. This will take some time, but maybe we can spend it in the mountains. Are you ready for another summer in Highridge, like last year?"

She had fond memories of their courtship. Morgan had fought an uphill battle getting her to go out with him in the first place, even though she had badly wanted to. Grandma's prejudice against summer people, who flocked to the North Carolina mountains for extended vacations in their huge mountain homes, had stood in the way of an easy relationship.

Hearing a knock on the door, Callie glanced up from Morgan's writing pad. Dorothy, Victoria, and Grandma had all gone home for the night, and Harry never knocked but blustered his way in.

The nurse opened the door and spoke to the guard. "Dianne Prescott. Says she's your aunt," she told them.

Morgan's eyebrows shot up, and he stared at Callie in silent communication.

"That's the first time she's claimed our relationship," Callie said.

Last summer had also been a traumatic time in Callie's life. Grandma had told her she'd lied about Callie's heritage. Callie's mother, Grandma's only child, had died in childbirth, but the father Callie had thought was also dead was alive, even though Grandma didn't know his whole name. Morgan had helped her find her biological father, P.J. Prescott, a summer person, who had loved her mother.

Dianne Prescott, an uppity socialite, was P.J.'s much younger sister. She'd had no use for Callie, whom she'd thought of as an ignorant mountain girl. P.J.'s mother had been downright hostile. But once Callie had married Morgan, or Trey as Dianne and her mother called him, they had been nicer, if not patronizing. P.J. had tried to make amends to Callie, and they were still working on a rather shaky relationship.

He had called Callie at home last night and reminded her that he, too, had broken his jaw last summer and assured her that Morgan would be fine. "He'll be drinking his meals for a while, then graduate to food from the blender, but that won't last long," P.J. had told her.

Callie had told Grandma about P.J.'s phone call.

"You can't swing a cat around here without hitting someone who's had a broken jaw," Grandma had said.

Even the guard at Morgan's door boasted that his jaw had once been broken.

"Do you want to see Dianne?" Callie now asked and Morgan shrugged in answer. She motioned for the guard to let her in.

"Trey, I came as soon as I could. I just got back into Atlanta today." Dianne rushed to his bedside with barely a glance in Callie's direction. "Oh, Trey, what's happened to you?" she moaned.

Callie wished she'd denied Dianne admittance. They had all kept an upbeat attitude around Morgan. Her negativism wasn't needed, especially now when he was worried about the trachea tube.

"He's doing much better," Callie said. "In a few weeks he'll be as good as ever."

"Is it true you won't ever sing again?" Dianne asked Trey.

"Dianne! Morgan can't speak right now, but the tube comes out tomorrow. It's time for you to leave. Visiting hours are over." Callie ushered her to the door and returned to Morgan's side.

"I'm sorry I let her in. Will she ever change?" Callie stared at the frown lines etched on Morgan's brow and leaned down and kissed them. "You're going to be fine," she said and smiled. "Now, are you ready for some sleep? Tomorrow's a big day."

ᴥ

Morgan spent a fitful night. He took one pain shot at Callie's insistence, but it didn't calm the anxiety in his eyes. Twice in the night Callie heard him try to breathe through his nose, then quickly uncover his trachea tube and suck in air.

"I'm sorry you had a bad night here," he wrote on his note pad at first light. "I'm ready now." He pointed at his tube.

"I know you've wrestled with it. Did you turn it over to God?" Callie had prayed through the night that Morgan could deal with the procedure.

"I'm okay now," Morgan wrote.

A little after seven the doctor came in. "Ready, Trey? I normally remove trachea tubes in one of the emergency rooms, but your manager is throwing a fit around here about security. Are you sure you're not the President of the United States?"

Morgan smiled, that little lift at the corner of his wired mouth.

"Let's do it," the doctor said, and the nurse helped Morgan sit in a hard chair for the procedure.

Callie stood in the corner and prayed. She looked up when Morgan took a loud breath through his nose.

"Not too bad," he said in a garbled voice through his wired jaws. His next distorted words let her know the agony he'd been suffering silently. "But can I sing?"

three

Morgan's eyes slowly opened as Harry entered the room. He didn't think he had the strength to sit up as his manager and the nurse commanded. But it was time to go.

Harry had made the decision to move him home at midnight. That way reporters wouldn't expect it, the halls would be empty, and there would be no pictures of a bruised and battered Trey in the morning papers.

Morgan would have clenched his teeth as he sat up, if his wired jaws had permitted it. As it was, he slowly straightened, took the two steps to the wheelchair, and fell into the seat.

This was no good. He wasn't an invalid; only his face was damaged. His legs were fine, if only he had the energy to move. He had to build up his blood. He'd have to force that liquid iron down, but it tasted horrible and stayed in his mouth for a long time after he swallowed what he could. A straw didn't work well, a syringe didn't shoot it down his throat, so he held a spoon up to the narrow slit between his lips and sipped. But as he was wheeled down the silent corridor, he vowed to take that iron eight times a day if necessary. He wanted to be back on his feet and now.

Morgan had never been a patient in a hospital before, and the experience was not one he wanted to repeat. The helplessness and feeling of being out of control of his life were taking their toll. Maybe returning home would somehow restore his ability to make decisions for himself.

"Where's Callie?" he asked as the elevator doors shut

the trio in the confined space. He needed his beautiful blond-haired wife with him. She gave him strength.

"She's at home. I told her I didn't want any wayward reporter who might be watching the house to follow her to the hospital."

"Too paranoid. We not this careful." He knew his speech wasn't clear. The wires made him unable to open his mouth. He mumbled at best in a shorthand language. Talking hurt, and the sound that came out wasn't his voice.

His agent shook his head. "Since your wedding and that video, everyone knows Callie's face. And now, both your picture and hers have been on the major networks every night since it happened."

Morgan nodded. He hadn't watched TV. He wasn't left alone enough to need the distraction. If Callie wasn't with him, his mother or Victoria or Grandma had been there. Plus the nurse. He'd been lucky to get a few naps in during the day. At home it would be different.

Harry wheeled him out to the car, and Morgan climbed in the front seat.

"Thank you," he told the nurse. He wouldn't be needing a nurse from now on. He had Callie and Wilda at home. And he'd soon be able to get around on his own.

❧

The trip home was much slower than the ambulance trip to the hospital had been. When Harry pulled into the long driveway, Morgan could see the lights of the house, from nearly every window, blazing a welcome.

Yellow ribbons were tied on the ornate columns that held up the veranda roof. A banner, WELCOME HOME, MORGAN, was stretched between two columns and flapped in the night breeze.

Callie stood in the open doorway with his mother and

family members behind her. Even Victoria's kids were there, despite the late hour.

Callie ran to the car and helped him out. He needed her strength as he walked toward the front door. Love radiated from the people inside, and it gave him the energy to smile, which stretched his lips to the hurting point.

Each took a turn hugging him, and then as if reading his thoughts and his need for rest, his family and Harry left. Grandma excused herself and went to the bedroom suite Callie had decorated for her frequent visits. Wilda went to her apartment, which was off the kitchen wing.

Morgan leaned on Callie and walked with her to their bedroom. His side of the king-sized bed held four pillows arranged in a slanting fashion that resembled the slope of his hospital bed. He crawled in and waited for Callie to join him.

"I need this," he said and reached out for her. Immediately, she took her rightful place in his arms. "I love you, honey."

"Oh, Morgan," Callie said. She choked back a sob, then let the silent tears fall.

"Tears, Callie?"

"I'm sorry. You should be the one crying, not me." She sniffed. "I'm being a big baby, but I'm so relieved to have you home."

Morgan squeezed her shoulders and made an attempt to kiss her on top of her head. He sighed, an exasperated sound. He'd increase that iron to twenty times a day. He had to get well and fast. He needed Callie as his wife.

"I can kiss you," Callie said. "At least on the forehead." She brushed his hair out of the way and kissed him.

Morgan made a choking sound. "Not had in mind," he mumbled.

Callie laughed and swiped at her tears. He was glad to see her mood swing the other way.

"You'll be well before you know it, honey. And the best thing for you is a good night's sleep."

But that night Morgan slept fitfully, and each time he shifted on the mound of pillows, Callie woke up.

"Maybe sleep on couch," he told her the next morning.

"Not on your life. I'm so glad to have you home, I don't care if I'm up all night long." She gave him a big hug. "Now you stay here. I'll bring you some breakfast."

But Morgan insisted in sitting in a reclining chair in the den. He sipped his liquid meal and made notes on a yellow legal pad. He didn't know what was happening at the office. Today was Thursday. The board of directors would be meeting in two days. He should be there.

"Walk outside," he told Callie before lunch time. If he condensed his sentences to few words, he didn't hurt so much when he talked.

"You do need exercise, and it's a glorious day out." Callie helped him toward the side door, but Morgan stopped still and motioned toward the french doors that led to the swimming pool.

"Are you sure you want to go out there?" she asked.

He nodded.

With slow, careful steps, and resting a lot of his weight on her, he walked to the pool house. The filter lid had been repaired and the filter now hummed softly. No water leaked from the rim.

He stared at the tiled floor where he'd fallen, but saw no telltale blood stains. He pointed at the spot and raised puzzled eyes to Callie.

"Yes, that's where you hit. The water from the filter diluted the blood, then Wilda cleaned up the rest that night.

Morgan, the doctor asked what made the wound in your neck, but I didn't know. Do you?"

He reached for the toolbox and extracted the needle-nosed pliers he'd used to tighten the bolt.

Callie shook her head. "You were very lucky the jab didn't do more damage. It was the blunt trauma that caused a separation of one vocal chord, but it should reconnect to the cartilage in eight or ten weeks. Until it does, you'll be real hoarse. Does it hurt to talk?"

He nodded. "Sing?"

"I'm sure you will. Just a matter of time. Let's go in," Callie suggested. She didn't mention that there was a chance the vocal chord wouldn't reconnect all the way. The odds were in his favor that it would, and she wasn't going to give him more to worry about.

"What caused?" He motioned to the filter.

"Ah. The pool men have an answer for that, but one of them wants to tell you himself. Do you want to talk to him today?"

Morgan nodded. More than anything he wanted to make sure this wouldn't happen again. Callie could have been the one out there when it blew.

&

Wayne Degraffenreid, the pool man, arrived a half-hour after Callie called. When Morgan saw his face, he thought Wayne must still be in his teens.

Callie sat beside Morgan's recliner while the young man shifted from one foot to the other. "Please sit down," Callie said.

"No, thank you. I just need to say this." He took a deep breath, then another. "Okay. I'm the one who caused your accident. I put the wrong size of bolt on the lid. The old one was rusted, and I put a new one on, but I didn't have one big enough. I didn't know it would matter, and I wanted it to look good for you. I'm so sorry."

"How long work with company?" Morgan asked.

"I worked for them a little over a month. But the company isn't to blame. It's me. I should have known better." He ran his fingers through his dark hair and heaved a big sigh. "I want to pay for the damages and your hospital bills. It'll take me a while. I can pay you some each month."

"Don't need money," Morgan said.

Callie stood and walked toward the young man. "Do you still work for them?"

"No," he said, looking down at his shoes. "They fired me when this happened."

"Where do you work now?"

"I'm looking for something else. I'll find work. I'm a good worker. I just made a mistake. I wouldn't hurt you for anything," he apologized again. "I've always admired your music. I wish it had been me and not you."

Morgan could see in the young man's eyes that he was sorry. "Call you," he said, then looked at Callie.

"We'll call you," Callie told the pool man. "Thank you for coming." She walked him to the door then returned to Morgan.

He was on his feet and walking toward his study.

"Can I get you something, Morgan?"

"Come," he said.

Callie followed and watched him find a number in his address book.

" 'Vestigate," he said.

Callie looked at the name and recognized it as the private investigator Morgan had hired to find her father. The PI hadn't found him, but he had eliminated a couple of possibilities.

"You want him to investigate the pool man?"

Morgan nodded.

"Why?"

"Find what kind of person," he said.

"Okay," Callie said and reached for the phone. Morgan sat in his desk chair and listened to the conversation and nodded in satisfaction.

"Now, Morgan," she said after she replaced the receiver, "you need to rest. Harry will be over at one, and Charlie's coming at three. I think I'm becoming your secretary."

"No. Wife," Morgan said and pushed himself out of the chair. He placed his arm around her and pulled her to his side. "Need you. Need iron."

"It's not time for your medicine."

"Take more," Morgan said. "Get strong." He patted her on her behind.

Callie looked into Morgan's teasing eyes and laughed.

"What's going to make you strong is plenty of food and more exercise. You've lost weight, and Grandma and Wilda are determined to get it back on you. You get to graduate to blender food today, and they've been cooking up a storm this morning. I think there's some kind of unspoken contest."

She walked with him, his arm still around her, to the kitchen and pulled out a chair for him. Grandma and Wilda were already at the table, drinking coffee.

"Phillip said his favorite food when his jaw was broken was beef stew, puréed of course." She called her father Phillip, because that's what Grandma had said her mother had called him. "So, Wilda's made that. And on the corner burner," she said, sounding a little like a boxing announcer, "we have Grandma's chicken and homemade noodles."

"Are you hungry, Morgan?" Grandma asked. "I'll fix

you up just right." The spry old woman got to the blender before Wilda could get out of her chair.

"Two courses," Morgan said.

"You want to try them both?" Callie asked.

He nodded. He'd eat anything they fixed for him. And he'd eat plenty of it, even though it took him a while to eat.

❧

The afternoon tired Morgan. First Harry visited, purely social, but Morgan could tell something was on his mind. Then Charlie met with him in his study.

While the two men discussed Rutherford Group business, Callie lay down. She could sympathize with Morgan's frustration with his tiredness. She had been up with him in the night, which hadn't helped, but she knew the depth of her tiredness stemmed from another source.

She had kept her Monday morning doctor's appointment, letting Grandma and Dorothy stay with Morgan in the hospital. She knew they thought she'd gone home to rest, but she'd driven straight to the doctor's office and spent an anxious few minutes waiting for the test results.

She had considered a home pregnancy test, but wanted to be absolutely positive and start on vitamins or whatever she needed to make sure her baby was healthy. Having heard stories about inconclusive results from too early testing, she had waited an extra week before going in for the test.

When the nurse had called her into an interior room, Callie didn't want to go. She had lived with the secret hope for a few weeks, and she didn't want to destroy her dream. Slowly, she'd followed the nurse into the room.

"Congratulations. According to the information you gave us with your blood sample, your baby's due December fifth, give or take a week or two. We're more accurate than the weatherman, but not by much."

Callie knew she had grinned from ear to ear, not at the nurse's joke, but at the joy of being pregnant. She was going to have Morgan's baby! "Thank You, God. Thank You," she had whispered. She had picked up vitamins before going back to the hospital to see Morgan, but she hadn't told him her news.

She wanted to tell him now, but she didn't want him to worry about her when he should focus on getting well.

They had talked about having children, and he had confided that he wanted a houseful, but he didn't want her to go through the delivery. Since her mother had died in childbirth, and Grandma had given birth to four stillborn babies, he had transferred those thoughts to her.

Callie had assured him that Grandma probably hadn't had good prenatal care and that her mother had suffered from a hemorrhage that sometimes affected young mothers; neither were inherited conditions. She had no fears herself, but she knew Morgan hadn't been convinced that she wouldn't be putting herself at risk if she became pregnant.

No, she couldn't tell him now. For the moment he had too much to handle. She saw the fear in his eyes whenever his singing career was mentioned. She saw frustration whenever he thought of the Rutherford Group. She loved him too much to add one more worry to his load. She'd wait and tell him as soon as he was well.

Morgan had not performed live on stage since the benefit he had given for the church. He'd never liked performing live and together they had decided he shouldn't have to give concerts. However, he still intended to continue his studio recording. But had that choice been taken from him now? Of course his hoarse voice sounded different. She knew she shouldn't judge it on the mumbled partial sentences that he muttered, but the nagging thought stayed in her mind. What was it doing to Morgan?

She rolled over on her back and stared at the ceiling and rested her hand on her stomach, wondering about the child inside her. Was it a boy or girl?

In about seven months she would have a son or daughter. What kind of mother would she be?

That thought sent her mind to her new friend—Jeff's mother. She sat up and reached for the phone. Marie Richardson answered after the first ring.

"I walked down to Morgan's room this morning and saw he was gone. Did you get him out without reporters? How's he doing?"

Callie was impressed that Marie could ask about Morgan when her son lay partially paralyzed in bed. He was out of danger, but had a long road to recovery ahead of him. They still did not know if he would ever walk again. Time alone would tell.

"He's tired, but he's glad to be home. When Jeff gets out, we hope you'll bring him over. Morgan wants to meet him, even though it wasn't possible at the hospital."

She shivered at the thought of the hospital. Now that they were home, it seemed like another world. How did doctors and nurses see injured and diseased people day after day and go on without their hearts breaking with each case?

She finished her conversation with Marie, slipped her shoes on, and went to Grandma's room.

"You're leaving?" she asked as she gazed at the opened suitcase on the bed.

Grandma smiled and continued packing. "Now that I've made enough chicken and noodles to last Morgan a week,

I reckon my usefulness is done for now. Wilda said she'd drive me back home. Morgan needs privacy now that he's here."

"Grandma, you're part of our family. You know that."

"I know that, Callie Sue. And I know that man needs to hold you every minute he can, and he doesn't need an audience."

"Grandma!"

"While we're talking heart to heart, here's somethin' I want to know. When are you goin' to tell him about the baby?"

four

Callie's mouth flew open, and Grandma chuckled.

"How did you know?" Callie asked.

Grandma chuckled again. "I've seen a mighty lot of pregnant women in my life, and they all have that same little secret smile. Even with Morgan laid up like this, you still have it. Now, it had to be a baby. Otherwise, nothing would have made you smile."

Callie hugged Grandma and told her the due date. "I'm not going to tell Morgan until he's well. He doesn't need to worry about me while he's worried about singing again and how the company's doing without him."

Grandma nodded. "Probably wise. I'm happier than I can say for you. But now, I need to be getting out of here. You don't need Wilda this afternoon, do you?"

"No. She can take you home. I just wish you'd reconsider. We haven't had time for a proper visit."

"Why don't you bring Morgan to the mountains to rest? Clean air might do him good. Being away from that swimming pool might help, too."

"I've been thinking of suggesting that. After the board meeting on Saturday, I think he'll be content to keep in touch with the company via long distance."

Callie carried Grandma's suitcase to the front entry. Wilda scurried out of the kitchen and explained the supper situation. After a quick goodbye to Morgan, they were on their way to North Carolina.

As Callie turned away from the door, Charlie Lockhard

called to her from the doorway of the study. "Callie, would you come in here a minute?" Frown lines around his mouth signaled his mood.

Callie walked inside and saw the exhausted slump to Morgan's shoulders as he sat behind his desk. He looked at her as if she were a lifeline in a storm, and Callie stepped around the desk so she could put her arms on his shoulders.

"Please tell Morgan that he can't attend the meeting Saturday," Charlie began. "He'd be distracting, and we have a lot of ground to cover. I can handle the meeting. The agenda's been set for weeks."

Callie looked down at Morgan and saw the tiredness in his eyes. He'd sat at his desk while Harry was here and for almost an hour with Charlie. There was no way he could handle a day-long board meeting.

"Morgan, Charlie's right. You can't physically do that so soon. In another week, I'm sure you could. However, we can have a conference call on a speaker phone set up so that you can monitor the meeting from here. You can hear all that goes on there and write down any comments. I'll be here to speak your thoughts to board members. Technology will allow you to be there without being there. That won't be hard to set up, will it, Charlie? We'll need a couple of speaker phones in the board room so we can hear all the conversations."

"Consider it done."

Callie massaged the tightness in Morgan's shoulders. "We'll bring the recliner in here, so you can move back and forth when you get tired. We want all the handouts and charts here, too, Charlie."

"I'll personally deliver everything tomorrow."

"All right, Morgan? Will this work for you?"

Morgan nodded. When would this nightmare end? He was so tired. As much as he hated the pain medicine and the out of control feeling it brought, he thought he'd take some and lie down. Then maybe he could sleep for more than an hour.

Charlie arranged to come back the next afternoon, then left. Callie helped Morgan to bed.

"Harry upset," Morgan muttered.

"What about?" Callie asked. She had left Morgan alone with his agent, thinking she'd be in the way.

"Don't know," Morgan said. "Find out."

"Okay. You get some sleep. I'll be checking on you."

"Stay?" Morgan patted the bed beside him, and Callie lay down with her head on his chest. About fifteen minutes later, Morgan's breathing became regular, and Callie slowly shifted positions so she could get up without waking him.

In the quiet of Morgan's study, she punched the phone button that was programmed with Harry's number. After she got Harry on the line, Callie went straight to the problem.

"Morgan says you're upset. Why?"

Harry was silent for a long moment. "He's got to perform again. Live."

"Now, Harry, you know he's decided to give up concerts. He'll do more albums, though. I know he'll sing again. It's too important to him." She believed that. She had prayed about it and felt at peace. God had given Morgan a wonderful voice, one He wouldn't take away.

"The albums aren't enough," Harry growled in that way he had. "His fans have to see him. There's been too much publicity. Some of them probably believe he has no face, like that one article said. When he's well again, he's got to sing in public."

"You mean on a TV special? One that could be taped?"

"I mean in a come-back concert. This has to be big, Callie. It has to show everyone that Trey is back and better than ever. That he has conquered a tragedy and lived to sing about it."

"Aren't you a little melodramatic, Harry?"

"No. It's got to happen. And you have to make him want it."

"Me?"

"He'll do anything for you. And you have to want this for him. Believe me, Callie, it means his career. I've been in this business a long time, and I know what I'm talking about. Trey's fans have to see him perform live. Those who can't be there have to see him on videos in front of an audience, so they know there were no special camera angles to make him look good."

Callie twisted the phone cord in her hand. She hated to admit it, but what Harry said made sense. "I'm not going to push him on this now. He needs rest to recoup. He can't be worrying about anything else. He's already scared that he won't be able to sing again, even in a studio."

"He'll sing," Harry said matter-of-factly. "When can we push him on this concert?"

"After the wires come off. Six weeks, the doctor said. It may take longer for the vocal chord to reconnect, maybe eight weeks. Give him time, Harry."

Harry grumbled, but agreed. After he hung up, Callie walked outside to the pool and wandered around. If only Morgan had been another two feet away from that filter when it blew. If only she hadn't put that plant so close to the edge, so that it fell in and clogged the filter with dirt and leaves. Guilt rushed at her.

She remembered that afternoon clearly when Wilda had

told her that plant was too close to the water. But Callie had insisted it was fine. If she hadn't moved it, the filter wouldn't have clogged.

She could go on and on with what-ifs, but she had to deal with reality. And a big reality was she felt responsible for the accident.

She walked back into the house and tiptoed to their bedroom. Morgan lay propped up on the pillows as she'd left him. She knew it wasn't a comfortable position for him. He liked sleeping on his stomach or his side. If only they could get back to normal. There was that phrase again. If only.

Morgan's face was healing. The deepest bruises around his eyes were still a brilliant red, but the darkest blue areas of two days ago were mustard yellow, and the yellow ones of yesterday were already lighter. Tomorrow the doctor was coming over to take out the stitches that ran from below his nose, through his lips, and all the way under his chin. Dr. Fuhr didn't normally make house calls, but he'd said he understood the pressures of unwanted publicity and would come to the house.

Morgan must have felt her presence, for he opened his eyes, looked at the ceiling, and then found her with his gaze.

"I'm sorry, Morgan," Callie said.

"Not wake me," he mumbled and shook his head.

Callie crossed the room and stood beside their bed. She had to say this. She prayed for courage to make her confession.

"I'm sorry I caused your accident," she choked out.

"You caused? No." He shook his head again.

She took a deep breath and knew what the pool man had gone through that morning. She should have spoken up then, but she had been too ashamed.

"If I hadn't placed that plant where the wind could blow it over, it wouldn't have clogged the filter and caused the water pressure to build up and the top to blow."

Morgan swung his feet to the floor and pushed himself off the bed. "Accident," he said and held out his arms to her.

For the second time in less than twenty-four hours, he held her as she sobbed. He made soothing noises through the wires.

"This hard on you," he said. "Me, too, if it were you."

Callie sniffed and reached for a tissue from the night table. "Yes. It's hard. And I'm sorry for the accident, and I'm sorry for falling apart when you need me."

"Need you to cry for me," Morgan said. "Need you to care." He ran his hands over her back and pulled her closer. "I love you."

"I know. And I love you more than I can ever tell you."

She went up on her tiptoes to kiss him, and he bent down. When she reached for his forehead, he shook his head.

"On lips."

"Oh, Morgan, I don't want to hurt you." But his eyes told her he needed loving, so she gently brushed her lips against his.

"Need take iron," he said. "More iron."

Callie smiled and dried her tears. She knew what he was talking about, and her heart was glad that he loved and desired her.

"Your mom will be over a little later," Callie said. At that moment the phone rang, and she reached for the receiver. Morgan didn't let her move from his side.

"Hi, Phillip," she said as soon as she recognized her father's voice.

Morgan's eyebrows lifted and Callie nodded.

Phillip had called a couple of times since Morgan had been hurt. In the past, Phillip's few calls from Boston had been strained. For Callie, trying to develop a relationship with a man she hadn't known existed until last summer wasn't easy.

Morgan had helped track down her father with the sketchy information Grandma had given her. He was a summer person who had gone to the mountains for vacation. Callie's mother, Daisy, had called him Phillip on the day she had died in childbirth, but Grandma didn't know his last name. She had seen him once in town and described him as tall with dark hair and around twenty.

Although Morgan had hired a private investigator, he had discovered Callie's father had been right on Regal Mountain where Morgan had a home. Until last summer, Phillip had not returned to the mountains since that fateful summer when he'd met Daisy. His mother had destroyed Daisy's letters to him in Boston and told him the love of his life had married someone else.

But now Callie had met her father, and they needed time to get to know each other before they could begin to form the bond of father and daughter. Phillip and his children had attended the wedding, but that was six months ago, and since then Morgan and Callie had been busy making their life together and establishing a new routine.

"He's much better," Callie was saying now to her father. "Getting stronger every day."

"Go to mountains," Morgan muttered. "See Phillip."

"Just a minute, Phillip." Callie looked at Morgan. "You want to go to the mountains after the board meeting? Stay there until your wires come off?"

He nodded, and she relayed the information to Phillip.

"That would be wonderful," she said. She covered the receiver. "He'll come to the mountains soon."

Morgan smiled and nodded.

"Yes. He's had some of your recommended beef stew," Callie said into the phone. "He loved it. He's having it for supper, too. And breakfast tomorrow. Okay. I'll tell him. Thanks for calling, Phillip." She hung up the phone. "He says you'll be back to normal in no time. He's coming to the mountains in another week or so and says he'll stay a couple of weeks until he has to get back for the summer school session at Boston U. We're going to talk about my mother."

Morgan squeezed her shoulders. "Work from mountains. Charlie in charge like last summer."

"Thank you, Morgan. I do want to know my father."

He nodded. "Eat?"

"Hungry again? Good. Because you eat so little at a time, you need to eat more frequently. What will it be? Instant Breakfast, stew, or chicken and noodles?" Again she fixed all three and watched Morgan sip his food.

When Dorothy came, she brought puréed barbecued beef. "It's really watered down to get the chunks out, but I tasted it, and the flavor's still there," she said.

Victoria and the kids came over and brought Morgan's favorite chocolate ice cream, and for a snack he had a malt.

🍂

That night Morgan slept fitfully again, but he had at least a few hours rest. The pain wasn't so bad now, but his sleep was disturbed by the uncomfortable position in which he needed to lie. Each time he unconsciously turned his face to the side, the wires would push on his jaw and awaken him.

On Friday, Morgan stayed up longer in the recliner and found he could snooze in it better than in the bed. Harry delivered a large bag of get-well cards from fans. Callie opened them and read him the funny ones. Charlie brought over the material for the board meeting. And the doctor took out the stitches.

That evening, Morgan experienced some flashbacks of the accident. He tried not to communicate his anxiety to Callie. When she sent searching looks his way, he smiled as best he could with the wires restricting movement.

"Seems odd that our lives could be so altered in such a short period of time," she said.

Morgan's keyed up energy allowed him to walk the perimeter of their grounds with Callie. After the exercise, he was worn out and that night he slept better.

The board meeting was scheduled to begin at nine. Charlie called at eight-thirty and left the speakers on the phone so Morgan could hear the greetings and noise of the board members and the company executives who would be presenting reports.

Callie sat in Morgan's chair. On the desk was a cup of coffee, which Wilda kept filled, and the same rolls that were being served in the board room. Wilda had made some lemon pudding for Morgan, and he smiled at the pretend world that she and Callie had set up for him.

The meeting went smoothly with Callie reading Morgan's opening remarks and Charlie taking over the meeting after that. Morgan scribbled comments on his legal pad, and Callie voiced them to the board.

During the noon break, Morgan took a nap. During the afternoon session, he sipped food and listened intently.

At the end of the meeting, Callie read a statement about Morgan being in the mountains for the next five weeks and designating Charlie as the one in charge at the corporate offices.

"Morgan will be in touch daily by phone. There will be no break in the regular chain of command, except that it may take a little longer to get decisions made."

"Went well," Morgan said, after the phone connection had been broken.

"Yes. Now, when shall we leave for the mountains?" They kept clothes at the mountain house so they didn't need to pack.

"Now?"

"Oh, you aren't up to that are you?" She glanced at her watch. "It'd be eight before we could get there."

"Go," Morgan said.

Callie found Wilda and told her they were leaving for a few weeks, then she gathered up medicines, placed Morgan's puréed foods in a cooler, and they left for their mountain home.

five

The drive to Highridge lifted Callie's spirits. As tired as she was after the long board meeting, she wanted to see the mountains again. She glanced at Morgan, who sat in the passenger seat, his gaze drifting along the scenic road.

She knew spring was his favorite season, and the middle of May had to be about the best time of spring. The trees had leafed out and overhung the two-lane road in places, forming a canopy overhead. The shades of green were fresh and clean, not the dried dusty green of late summer, and Callie was reminded of God's promise of rebirth. She prayed that Morgan, too, would be regenerated by being around nature instead of the concrete of the city.

As they neared Eagle Mountain, the road climbed, turned back on itself, and climbed again. Knowing the road as well as she did, Callie skillfully maneuvered the car.

They had stayed in their new home on Eagle Mountain on several weekends, but they hadn't been there for any extended length of time. Grandma had owned Eagle, and her house rested at the foot of the mountain. She'd given the land to Callie and Morgan for a wedding present. Building had begun on the house before they were married, and the interior had been completed three months ago.

A house of her own was a dream come true for Callie. Not that the Atlanta house wasn't hers, too, but it held Morgan's history. This one would have shared memories.

Callie had wanted Grandma to live in the new house, but Grandma had said her home was at the bottom of Eagle. It was a ramshackle old farmhouse that Callie had fixed up after she had gotten a job as an accountant. Although homey, it was a far cry from the mansion on the mountain.

Something niggled at Callie's mind. What had she forgotten to bring with them to the mountains? She went over the list in her head. Morgan's medicines, her own vitamins—those were of primary importance.

"Oh, no. I forgot to call Marie Richardson and check on Jeff."

"You can call from the house," Morgan said.

Callie nodded. The call would be longdistance, but she had quickly become accustomed to the luxuries of having money.

Had it changed her? she wondered. What had happened to the young girl who had received the first college scholarship financed by Trey, the country singing sensation? Was she still inside Callie? She hoped so. That was the girl Morgan had fallen in love with. She shook her head. Strong values, knowing right and wrong, a steadfast belief in God—those things were within her. Knowing she could reach for the phone and call anywhere in the world anytime she wanted didn't change her basic character.

The junction of the highway onto the county road loomed ahead. Callie turned and drove two miles into the country before Grandma's house appeared. Grandma sat in an old rocker on the front porch. She didn't seem surprised when they drove up.

"Welcome back," she called and walked out to the car and stood by Morgan's open window. "How you doing, Morgan?"

"Okay," Morgan mumbled.

Callie ran around the car and hugged Grandma. "We'll be staying a few weeks," Callie announced.

"Good. Do you both a world of good. You need anything up at the house?" She peered in the back seat and obviously saw nothing. "Groceries?"

"I'll run into Highridge tomorrow morning. Maybe you could stay with Morgan while I do?"

"Sure."

"Don't need babysitter," Morgan protested.

Callie leaned in the window and kissed him lightly on the lips. "Yes, you do. Humor me for just another week. Then I'll let you be alone. Promise."

Morgan nodded.

Callie gave Grandma another hug. "I want to get Morgan settled. See you tomorrow."

She climbed back into the car and started up Eagle Mountain. The road was steep with switchbacks every little bit, but the mountain wasn't as tall as Regal where Morgan's summer home was and where her father's parents had a home. Morgan had decided to keep the Regal Mountain home for his family to enjoy. Dorothy and Victoria's family used it regularly.

Near the top of the mountain, Callie glimpsed her home, nestled among trees. She caught her breath as she did each time she saw it. Viewed from below, the cathedral-type structure soared into the sky, with a floor-to-ceiling glass opening onto a large balcony. As she turned on the switchback, Callie lost sight of the house until she came out on top of the mountain. From this side, the high-pitched roof allowed the house to fit into the tall trees around it.

Callie pushed a button and the garage door opened. As soon as she'd parked the car inside, she helped Morgan into the house. They walked through the large kitchen and straight to the long windows. Callie opened one set of doors and seated Morgan on the balcony overlooking a fantastic view.

"Stay here. I'll get you something to eat and bring it out." She went back to the car for the cooler and their medicine bag, then warmed Morgan's puréed stew in the microwave.

She made a mental note to move the recliner out on the balcony for Morgan in the morning. She doubted he'd be up too much longer tonight. He'd been sitting most of the day.

She popped the top of a diet soda and carried it and Morgan's stew out on the deck.

"Glad we came," Morgan said.

"Me, too. There's nothing like these mountains to put life in perspective, is there? We're going to be fine, Morgan. I know it."

He nodded and sipped his supper.

Callie slipped inside, called the hospital, and talked briefly with Marie. Jeff was improving daily. He should be able to go home within a week.

"Morgan, you never got to meet Jeff," Callie said when she returned to the deck. "What do you think of having him and his parents here for a weekend? It would give him something to look forward to. He's quite a fan of yours."

"You like him?"

"Yes. He's a real fighter. He was injured so badly, but he doesn't give up. Did I tell you his accident was a result of a drunk driver? A hit and run, except the drunk also hit a tree at the end of the street, and that stopped him."

"Not say much about him."

"I guess I haven't told you his whole story. Of course, I've been so concerned about you and the board meeting. Doesn't that seem in a different world? That's what I love about the mountains. Cares seem to be as far removed as a rock at the foot of the mountain that's too little to be seen from here."

Morgan put his empty cup on a side table.

"You're tired aren't you? Give me five minutes to put fresh sheets on the bed and we'll lie down."

❧

One entire east wall of the bedroom was windows, just like in the living room. The bed faced them, so the first thing Callie saw when she awoke the next morning was the pink glow of the morning sunrise. She glanced over at Morgan who was still asleep on his hill of pillows.

He hadn't stirred much last night. Callie didn't know if it was due to his exhaustion or to the fresh mountain air.

She'd slept, too, and dreamed about their baby and the day when Morgan would be well. She would tell him about the baby the day the wires came off. Having that goal in mind made it easier for her to stand the wait.

Today she felt ready to face the world. She quietly made her way to the kitchen and made a pot of coffee. When she carried half a cup to Morgan, he was awake.

"Beautiful," he said.

"I know. I can't get enough of the view."

"Not view, you," he said with adoration in his eyes.

Callie laughed. "Flattery will get you a second cup of coffee if you can sip this one. I've let it cool a little bit for you. We need milk before I make you an Instant Breakfast. How about some chicken and noodles?"

Morgan nodded.

While Morgan bathed, Callie fixed his puréed meal.

"Take shower 'morrow," he told her later.

"I'll bet you'll be strong enough then that I won't worry about you standing in the shower."

"Sound like baby. Easy this way. I talk normal again?"

She knew he was worried that he'd get so accustomed to his verbal shorthand that he wouldn't form complete sentences ever again.

"Of course you will. There's no need for you to strain yourself any more than necessary. As long as we communicate, that's all that matters."

"You go store. I okay."

"Please, Morgan, humor me. Let Grandma come up for a little while. She hasn't gotten to visit with you, and it'll make her feel needed. In a couple of days, you can go to town with me."

A guarded look came into his eyes, and Morgan shook his head in a negative manner.

"We'll wait a while, then," Callie said. She called Grandma and set up a Morgan-sitting time.

Morgan walked slowly to the long windows and looked toward town, which was several miles to the north. Although Highridge was a wealthy resort town accustomed to celebrities and therefore didn't make a fuss over them, he knew his bruised face would cause stares and comments. He had tried on sunglasses and liked the way they hid the heavy bruises around his eyes, but they didn't disguise the jagged line on his face. Someone in Highridge would recognize him and tell the press he was here, and then the reporters would descend. No, he'd stay on the mountain until he was himself again.

Morgan turned to watch Callie while she talked. The morning sun shone off her honey gold hair, which she'd been letting grow longer because he'd asked her. His heart was warmed that she wanted to please him. She was a beautiful woman, and she was his wife. He thanked God that he'd met this woman who loved him as much as he loved her.

"It's all arranged. I'll leave you here alone long enough to drive down and bring her back. She said she'd walk up, but it's a steep climb for me. Grandma doesn't need to make it. Anything special you want from town?"

"Ice cream."

"Of course. I'll get tons of it."

Callie moved the recliner out on the deck and laid one of Grandma's crocheted afghans beside it in case Morgan got cold in the early morning mountain air. She walked beside Morgan as he carried a book out on the balcony and sat down.

"I'll be back before you can say Jack Robinson," Callie told him.

"Jack Wobinson," Morgan said, then took a sharp breath. He couldn't say *r*s. Was it because of the wires or his restructured palate?

"Don't worry," Callie said. "As soon as the wires come off you can open your mouth and yell Jack Robinson so that it echoes off Regal."

She was right. Surely she was right, he thought.

Callie leaned down and kissed him lightly on the lips. He put his arms around her and held her close for a moment before he let her go. As soon as she got back, he'd ask her to sit with him. He wanted to hold her and have her hold him.

With a wave, Callie left, and a short time later Grandma walked out on the porch.

"Well, Morgan, it's you and me," she said. "Want to play dominoes?"

That was Grandma's game, and Morgan knew he didn't stand a chance at winning. But he agreed to play. They sat down at the small round table in the kitchen. A game table was in the den, but Grandma always preferred the kitchen, so Morgan accommodated her. He accommodated everything Grandma wanted, since she meant so much to Callie. He loved the old woman, too, but he knew Grandma had the upper hand in their relationship.

Callie made her way slowly down Eagle Mountain for the second time in the last ten minutes. She slowed at her old home and marveled that she no longer lived there, but at the top of the mountain. What changes the last year had brought.

She touched her stomach and thought of the baby. Not telling Morgan was so hard. Luckily she'd had no morning sickness or any of the other discomforting side effects of early pregnancy. She'd read the pamphlets the nurse had given her, but she wanted to pick up a book on pregnancy. She'd call Morgan's doctor in Atlanta and cancel her own doctor's appointment there. Dr. Doody in Highridge could see them both while they were in the mountains. On Monday she'd take care of those details.

She drove directly to the grocery store. She didn't want to be gone long. Today she'd get only the necessities and make a longer trip during the week. She'd get Grandma to sit with Morgan again, although she knew he'd object. What she needed was an invisible babysitter, someone he was so used to, that he wouldn't think about her being there just to watch him. She needed someone like Wilda, but she couldn't ask her to come to Highridge for several weeks. She had a life in Atlanta, and besides, they needed someone house-sitting while they weren't staying there.

Because they hadn't stayed in the new house longer than a weekend, Callie hadn't thought of hiring a housekeeper for the mountain house. That would be the answer. Maybe Grandma would know someone. She sorted through the members of her church, but couldn't come up with someone who could work a full-time job for only six weeks, or maybe longer since it would be summer soon.

On a sudden impulse, Callie stopped at a pay phone and looked up the number of the receptionist at the CPA firm where she had worked as an accountant before her marriage. Liz answered on the second ring and seemed delighted to hear from Callie. After assuring her that Trey was doing well, Callie asked if she knew of anyone in the community who would want a temporary job as a housekeeper/companion for a few weeks.

"Callie, this is just what my sister needs," Liz said, excitement coloring her voice.

"Jean?" Callie had met Liz's sister on a few occasions. She couldn't imagine why she'd want this type of position.

"Her husband died just after you moved to Atlanta."

"Liz, I'm sorry. I didn't know."

"It's okay. A heart attack. He went suddenly, leaving Jean with two teen-aged boys and needing a job. She's been substitute teaching, trying to work into the school system. But that's iffy work. Some days she's called and some days she's not. And school's about out. This would be a perfect answer for her. Let me call her, and I'll feel her out."

"All right. I'm not home right now, but I will be in half an hour. Have Jean call me if she's interested." Callie gave her the number and fairly flew into the store.

She loaded up on milk and ice cream, then pampered herself with a bag of chocolate kisses. Maybe it was a pregnancy craving, or maybe it was just her sweet tooth acting up. She wanted to buy several small bags, but settled for one giant-sized bag.

Callie made it home, unloaded, and got Grandma back

down the mountain before her grandmother's ride came to take her to church.

"Morgan's been on the prayer list," Grandma said before she got out of the car. "I'll tell them he's home for a spell. Do you mind if people call on you?"

"I think Morgan would like the concern," Callie said.

Jean's call came exactly a half an hour after Callie had talked to Liz. They talked briefly and arranged for Jean to begin the next morning.

For the rest of Sunday, Callie snuggled by Morgan's side. He seemed stronger and wanted her by him. They went on a walk around the top of the mountain, not a long one, but a tiring one. Then again, they snuggled side by side on the porch swing on the balcony.

Morgan seemed in good spirits. When his boyhood friend, Robert Garrigan, called, he mumbled across the phone lines, his first attempt at phone communication.

"This will work," he said to Callie a few minutes later. "I can talk to Charlie every day without you."

"Hey, don't forget you need me, mister," Callie teased, but she was glad he was gaining confidence and was talking in better sentences, too.

"Robert and Marilyn coming to mountains next weekend," he said.

"Great. Can't wait to see them. Will they be here long?"

"Three weeks this time, then they'll be back later in the summer."

Both Marilyn and Robert were summer people whom Callie had met last year. Robert wrote best-selling mysteries, and Marilyn was a stockbroker in New York. They had married a month before Callie and Morgan had walked down the aisle.

Callie's father was coming, their friends would be

here, Jeff and his parents might come to the mountains, and Callie had hired Jean to help her out with the house and Morgan. All in all, their recuperating stay in the mountains looked like a good time for all. Just what the doctor ordered.

six

Morgan sat on the deck with Callie, enjoying the late morning sunshine. Jean was in the kitchen, preparing some new puréed foods to give him a different taste treat. "Isn't she terrific?" Callie asked.

"She seems nice." He hadn't thought far enough ahead to think they'd need someone up here, but Jean did free them from household chores, so they could do things. If he could do things. Just trying to speak in complete sentences seemed to be all he could do. If he was going to communicate on the phone, he needed full sentences.

Last night some people from Callie's church had come by. He'd met them all last summer and worked with some on the benefit program he'd performed to earn money for much-needed repairs on the old building. They wanted to express their support and concern, and he had spoken in as normal a fashion as he could manage in his hoarse voice.

He was taking his iron supplement and eating every couple of hours, since he ate such small amounts at a time. With every minimeal he felt stronger. He knew he had a long way to go, but he was seeing progress and that was giving him hope.

And he needed all the hope he could muster. His moods swung like a pendulum. When others were around, they bolstered his spirits. When he was alone, even for a short while, he felt tired, no, exhausted, and depressed. Once when Callie had the radio on and he'd heard one of his songs, he'd felt like crying. The last time he'd cried was when his father had died. And the time before that was probably in third grade when he'd had a bad bike wreck.

He had to get a grip. He couldn't let Callie know how much he ached for a return to the good life—life before the accident. He would never again take for granted simple things: walking as far as he wanted, eating an apple, or making love to his wife.

"How about strawberries and cream?" Jean asked, pulling him out of his thoughts.

Callie pushed a table closer to Morgan's chair. "That sounds wonderful." Callie was delighted with Jean. The red-headed woman was petite, about her height, with sparkling eyes and a level head on her shoulders. Callie liked her immediately, and Morgan seemed to like her as well.

When Callie mentioned Jean's late husband, the brightness in her eyes hadn't faltered. "We had wonderful years, and I have great memories. He's gotten his heavenly reward. I wouldn't wish it away from him, even though I miss him." With an undefeated attitude, although Callie knew light housekeeping and helping her with Morgan weren't Jean's goals in life, she kept a happy smile on her face and a lightness in her step.

Callie guessed Jean to be in her late thirties or early forties. Her sons were fourteen and sixteen. They might be friends for Jeff if he got to come up for a weekend. She hadn't broached the subject to Marie Richardson, but she would this evening when she called the hospital. Besides getting Jeff into a different environment and giving him the boost of meeting a celebrity, Callie had an ulterior motive. She hoped Jeff's indomitable spirit could help Morgan. He grew despondent with the waiting game of recovery. She could see it in his eyes at unguarded moments, although she knew he was trying to hide it.

Meanwhile, she was hiding her pregnancy. She didn't like being secretive, but she didn't know what else to do. She wanted Morgan to celebrate the baby with her, not mope around worrying needlessly about her. And right now she thought that was what he would do. He had too much time on his hands, not much energy, and too much to think about.

"What would you like to do this morning, Morgan?" she asked when they had finished their snack.

"I'm going to set up office hours," he said. "That way Charlie can depend on me talking to him around ten, after the mail comes and manager reports are completed. Then in the afternoon I can call again around four to catch up on the events of the day."

"Excellent idea," Callie said. "While you do that, I thought I'd go into town to the library. I'll pick you up a mystery or two."

✦

They parted, Callie feeling easy with Jean in the house in case Morgan needed anything. She didn't plan on being in Highridge long and parked on Main Street by the bookstore. She didn't want a library book on pregnancy, since Morgan might be with her when she'd need to return it, and she had no intention of letting him see this book until she could tell him about the baby. After poring over the baby section, she chose a book and then browsed a moment in the children's section.

Someday soon she'd have a little one who'd want storybooks read to him at nighttime. Him? Was she thinking of their child as a boy? She really didn't care which gender it was. She'd heard other pregnant women say the important thing was a healthy baby, and that was exactly how she felt. She walked outside into the spring sunshine and looked down the street toward the candy store. Dare she indulge herself? She still had a few chocolate kisses left, but her supply was dwindling. This store was famous for its hand-dipped chocolates.

As she stood by the car debating, Joe Lowery walked out of the bank a few doors down. "Joe," she called. She'd met him at the University of North Carolina at Chapel Hill when she'd answered his note on the bulletin board asking for a rider to share gas to Franklin, a town only a few miles away. They'd become close friends, and whenever he'd been on business in Highridge, he'd come out to Grandma's for a visit and a meal.

When she called his name again, he turned and walked down the street toward her. "Callie Sue," he said when they met and hugged. "I expected you'd turn up here soon. How's Morgan?"

"Doing better. Thanks for your calls to the hospital. We've been busy or I'd have gotten back with you. What are you doing in Highridge?"

"Our bank has bought out the one here, so I'm liaison man right now, making sure the new procedures are in line with our policies. I may be moving here; it's all up in the air right now."

"Can you come out for supper tonight? I know Morgan would like to see you."

"Sure," he said without hesitation.

"Good. See you at seven."

Callie picked up some books from the library for Morgan and within an hour she was back on the mountain.

⁊⧫

Morgan had just walked outside for some exercise when he heard the motor pulling the car up the steep inclines of the mountain road. He chuckled. Callie had driven a manual shift pickup when he'd met her, but she'd never been smooth at shifting gears. He listened to the grind as she shifted to low in the sports car they'd driven from Atlanta. He should give her lessons on listening to the engine and knowing the exact moment to shift. He waited until she came around the last switchback and waved as she pulled into the garage.

She glanced guiltily at the seat beside her and leaned over before he could open the door for her. Was she hiding something from him? She climbed out and kissed him, then reached back in and picked up some books. She grabbed a sack, and he read the logo on the side. Now he understood what she'd been doing. "Callie, you don't have to hide candy. It doesn't bother me for you to eat in front of me."

Callie looked startled for a moment before she sighed. "Are you sure, Morgan? I couldn't pass the candy store without stopping in. Oh," she hurried on, "I ran into Joe and he's coming to supper. I'd better tell Jean. How was your call to Charlie?" She knew she was rambling, but he'd almost caught her with the baby book. She'd stuffed it under the passenger seat and would have to retrieve it later when he took a nap.

ða

Dinner that night was a huge success, Callie thought. She had missed contact with Joe, who reminded her of her single days at the university. He also had news of people in the Highridge community and filled her in on what was happening with the local people. Morgan seemed comfortable with Joe, although she remembered the first time they'd met, she'd thought Morgan was jealous. Morgan and Joe had gotten to know each other better during last summer's concert, and Joe had been one of the few invited to their secret marriage ceremony.

After dinner they sat on the balcony and talked some

more. Morgan listened politely, but he was tired and he was feeling sorry for himself. He knew he had told Callie that she could eat anything in front of him, but the steaks she and Joe had cooked on the grill for dinner had him salivating. He was hungry for real food—for a salad and hot rolls. He'd eaten some warmed up chicken casserole, puréed of course, that Jean had prepared before she'd gone for the evening. But even the chocolate malt Callie had fixed hadn't done away with the empty feeling he had inside.

After Joe had left and Callie was sleeping peacefully, Morgan quietly got up and fixed himself an Instant Breakfast. The silence in the house penetrated to his soul, and he sat in the dark living room and stared at the blackness outside the windows.

Why had this happened to him? Was there some divine plan he had no notion of? Was it a random act of cosmic violence? Why? Why? Was there a reason that could make sense of this?

In the wee hours of the morning, Callie reached out for Morgan and touched nothing. Alarmed, she crawled out of bed and called his name. She heard a soft mumble from the living room and found Morgan sitting in the recliner.

"Are you hurting?" she asked and kneeled beside him.

"No. Got hungry and ate. I'm hungry again. Hungry for you." He reached for her, and she climbed onto his lap.

Callie saw the adoring look in his eyes and knew her eyes reflected back the overwhelming love she felt for this man. She took the initiative and kissed him on the forehead, on his cheek, on his lips, on his neck. She hugged him close, then slid off his lap, and, taking his hands, led him to the plush rug in front of the fireplace. Man to woman, woman to man, they expressed their love.

"I have missed you so much," Morgan said.

"I know. Why is it that physical love makes us feel so

close? Has God made us fit together so perfectly because it makes us see ourselves as one? Makes us united in body as well as spirit?"

"Don't know," Morgan said. "Just know I love you so much."

"Come on, let's go back to bed," Callie said. "You need to get some rest."

"Feel rested now," Morgan said. "Feel whole again."

Callie laughed and arm in arm they walked back to the bedroom.

❧

The rest of the week fell into a routine. Morgan called his office as he'd planned. When he was closeted in his study, Callie read her baby book and felt guilty that she hadn't shared her joy with him. But she had made her decision to tell him when the wires came off, and she knew that was the best thing for Morgan.

She had taken Morgan to the doctor in Highridge. Dr. Doody had agreed to examine him once a week to ensure against infection and pain. A trip back to Atlanta wouldn't be necessary until it was time for the wires to come off. On another day, Callie saw the doctor by herself and was reassured that she was doing all the right things for her baby's health.

Jean was working out like a dream, and every day Callie liked her more. Her bubbly personality lightened the place, and she made it her mission in life to prepare tasty treats for Morgan.

Callie called Marie Richardson each day and got updated reports on Jeff's condition. Marie couldn't believe Callie and Morgan really wanted them to visit in the mountains, but after she'd talked the invitation over with her husband, they had decided to take them up on it. Jeff would be released from the hospital on Friday. He'd spend a week recovering at home, then Marie and Ken would bring him to the mountains for the weekend.

On Friday, Robert and Marilyn arrived from New York. They came directly to the house from the airport without stopping at their own house on Regal Mountain. Morgan laughed, more of an inward sound than an out loud sound, when he saw his best friend.

He and Robert had gone through a lot in their growing up years and, as men, had grown even closer. Robert wrote mystery novels, and when Morgan had needed help discovering who Callie's father was, he'd turned to Robert, thinking that if he could make his fictional detective, Sinclair, solve so many mysteries, maybe he could help with the mystery of Callie's father. Robert had been glad to help. His wife Marilyn was a wonderful person, too. She and Callie had formed a solid friendship bond.

Although Robert's eyes showed concern when Morgan first saw him, he didn't show pity but compassion. "Didn't I give you a black eye once back when we were around eight?" Robert asked as they all sat on the balcony with a big pitcher of lemonade. "It looked about like that."

"Wasn't it the other way around?" Morgan asked in his hoarse voice. "Didn't I give you one?"

"Maybe we both looked a little beaten up after the big fight," Robert said.

"What were you fighting about?" Callie asked. The two men looked at each other.

"Haven't a clue," Robert said.

"I can't remember, either."

"Probably some little blond," Marilyn teased. "They've always claimed to be big ladies' men. Even at eight, they must have been charmers."

Callie looked at the two friends and thanked God that they had come. Just that morning she had seen that look of despair in Morgan's eyes. He was so good at hiding it, or maybe it just came and went. She didn't know. And they didn't discuss it. When she'd asked him if anything was wrong, he'd said he was fine. Now he looked happy, his eyes shining with pleasure.

"What caused the accident?" Robert asked. "Can it happen to any pool filter?"

Callie explained what she knew of the problem and Morgan elaborated. "Investigator looking into background of pool man," he said.

"You think someone did this on purpose?" Marilyn said with a gasp.

"No. Just wanted to know about him. He was willing to pay for hospital bill," Morgan said. "He seemed very sorry."

"You know," Robert said thoughtfully, "this could be a plot for Sinclair. This could be made to look like an accident, but be carefully orchestrated. Could the blow have killed a person?"

"Morgan could have bled to death," Callie said and shivered involuntarily. "He lost a third of his blood. That's why he's still so weak. In another few days we should see major changes in his energy level."

"This has real possibilities. Do you mind if I enlarge it a bit and use it for a book? I could set the murder in an isolated place, say a mountain top in North Carolina," he said and looked around. "No close neighbors, no ambulance service. Hey, this could work."

"Well, good to know that I've provided a plot for you," Morgan said. "I knew there had to be some good come out of this."

Callie looked sharply at Morgan. Although he was teasing his friend, she heard a bitter ring in what he said, and for a brief moment that haunted look had returned to his eyes.

seven

"This will be good for you," Callie said and straightened Morgan's tie. "It's been two weeks now and you need to get out and see people. I wouldn't count one quick trip to Highridge to the doctor as getting out. Especially since you went in the back door and saw only Dr. Doody."

"They don't need to see me," Morgan mumbled. He'd let Callie talk him into going to church and now he was regretting that decision. "God understands why I'm not in church."

"I'm sure He does. But He'll be proud of you for making the effort, especially since He knows what it costs you."

Morgan took a deep breath. Several of the church members had been by in the last few days and had seen the way he looked. But a whole group was different than one or two at a time. They wouldn't gawk at him, would they?

Callie drove them to the bottom of Eagle in the van they kept at their mountain home. Grandma was going with them, and the little sports car wouldn't hold all three of them.

Grandma was waiting on her porch. She climbed aboard and the trio set off for the little country church where Callie and Morgan had been married.

The old church, dedicated in 1804, was as solid as the year it was built. The money that Morgan's concert had raised for the church had assured that. A shored-up foundation, a new roof, new windows, and a new coat of white stucco over repaired cracks made the church look brand new again.

No extra space had been added. It was still a small one-room church with a center aisle and antique pews on each side. But the fifty members didn't need special classrooms. They merely divided into Sunday school classes by sitting in different areas of the small sanctuary. A circuit preacher ministered to the church every other Sunday. This week there would be no sermon.

Morgan walked into the church wearing dark glasses to hide the worst of his bruises. He felt silly with them on inside the sanctuary, and although he didn't want to expose his face to curious looks, he took them off.

Around forty people stared at him for all of three seconds, just as they would anyone who entered and walked to the second pew.

"Glad to see you out, Morgan," one member said.

A couple of the teen-agers came over to him and told him how sorry they were that he'd been hurt.

From behind the podium, an elderly man called the Sunday school meeting to order. The combination secretary/treasurer read the minutes and gave the treasury balance. Then the congregation stood for a prayer followed by a hymn.

Morgan tried to sing. When he talked, he formed his words slowly so that he could be understood, but he couldn't keep up with the pace of the song, even though "In the Sweet Bye and Bye" wasn't sung at a fast clip. He knew the wires hampered him, but was that all? He tried humming along and heard his voice crack, and the hoarseness in his voice wouldn't go away.

As if reading his thoughts, Callie turned to him and smiled. "It will be all right," she said.

The Sunday school lesson was on the prodigal son, a

lesson that Morgan had never really understood.

". . .There will be more rejoicing in heaven over one sinner who repents than over ninety-nine righteous persons who do not need to repent," Tommy Ray read from the quarterly.

"That doesn't seem fair," Morgan spoke up. He had never questioned that before. He had merely accepted it. "Why should we live good lives if we'd be more celebrated if we led bad ones, then changed?"

A lively discussion of the parable ensued with Tommy Ray summing up the consensus. "The son who had worked the land with his father was reassured that his inheritance was his, and the son who had taken his inheritance and spent it wasn't going to get more. The prodigal son would have to live with what he'd done, but he was forgiven for it. Isn't that right?"

"Jesus said He had come to save sinners, not punish them, but that doesn't mean they won't be accountable for their actions in this life," another member spoke up.

"The whole thing is about forgiveness," Callie said. "And that's what we as Christians should dwell on."

The piano player started up a lively tune that signaled the end of Sunday school, and the members moved back to their regular seats for the closing hymn.

Over the Sunday dinner table at Grandma's, the discussion turned again to the prodigal son.

Grandma took her turn at explaining the parable. "I think living a good life gives its own rewards—like how others treat us and the good feeling we enjoy while we're on this earth. At the same time, we oughta forgive those who do what we think is wrong. We can't know what's in other people's hearts. We can only know what's in our own."

As Grandma said this, Callie looked at Morgan and

wished she knew more of what he was feeling.

ও

On Wednesday morning, Callie knew she was going to be sick. She felt it before she even raised her head from the pillow. With quick, purposeful movements she threw off the covers and dashed for the bathroom.

As soon as he heard her, Morgan was beside her, holding her head. He had been afraid that she'd have some sort of reaction to her father coming to the mountains. A nervous stomach hadn't crossed his mind, but here it was.

When Phillip had called earlier in the week to announce he'd be there on Wednesday, Morgan had watched Callie alternate between excitement and apprehension. They hadn't seen Phillip since the wedding, and now that they were going to have a couple of weeks in close proximity, Morgan realized she couldn't handle the uncertainty of what their relationship would be.

Grandma hadn't helped. She'd been as moody as Callie. Morgan had finally talked to Grandma about how important this was to his wife, and that they needed to play it up as a positive thing, not dwell on the negative. Grandma had sniffed and said she knew Morgan was right, but it was hard.

Now looking at a pale Callie, Morgan knew he'd underestimated what this first heart-to-heart encounter would be like for her.

"I'm all right," Callie said. She looked up at him with guilt in her eyes.

Why would she feel guilty about her sickness? It wasn't every day that a woman got to talk to a father she didn't really know about a mother she'd never met. Although the two had spoken on the phone several times, they had never broken down the barriers of the past. Today was the day.

Phillip had even mentioned it when he had called.

Morgan washed Callie's face with a cold washcloth. He felt odd taking care of her when she had been taking care of him. He'd been taking advantage of her, he realized, relying on her strength to carry him through this hard time. Well, she could depend on him to get her through her hard time.

He led her back to bed. "Can I get you some crackers and a soda?" That had been his mom's remedy for an upset stomach. Surely it would work for Callie. He'd never seen her sick before, and he didn't like seeing her lie there so helpless and pale.

"Crackers sound good. I'll be all right. I'm not really sick," she said.

"I know. But I'll stay right by you when he comes, Callie. We'll learn about your past together." He was stronger now. Two weeks and five days had gone by since the accident, and for the last few days he'd felt physically better and better. Emotionally he wasn't exactly solid, but maybe he'd been feeling sorry for himself. That wasn't his normal way, and he'd watch that in the future. "I'll get those crackers."

Callie couldn't believe that Morgan had misinterpreted her sickness, but she wasn't going to correct his mistake. She hoped this wasn't the beginning of a streak of morning sickness episodes. Grandma had said some pregnancies had isolated incidents, and she prayed this was one.

"Here you go." Morgan put a plate of saltines and a can of soda on the night stand. He gathered some throw pillows off the floor and piled them behind Callie's back so she could eat. He smiled that wired-mouth smile that Callie was getting used to. "You're going to be fine."

"I know. Thanks, Morgan. I love you so much," she said

and then dissolved into tears.

"Honey, it's going to be fine." Morgan climbed into bed beside her and pulled her into his arms. He stroked her hair as she nestled her head on his chest.

"I know. This is silly."

"No, it's not. Just nerves. You'll be fine."

In half an hour she was over the nausea—and found herself ravenous instead. Chocolates ranked high in her mind, but she settled instead for the toast and tea Morgan fixed her. He drank his ever-present Instant Breakfast.

Sunshine filtered through the leaves of the trees overhead and speckled the table on the balcony where they ate. A gentle morning breeze reminded her that it was still May, and Callie pulled a sweater closer around her.

"Shall we have lunch out here? It'll be warmer then, and I imagine Phillip would like the view."

"Good idea. I'll do my office stuff early, then we'll get everything ready," Morgan said.

Jean arrived, and she and Callie worked on a fruit salad in the kitchen. "He's probably as nervous as you," Jean said.

Callie had explained about not knowing her father and the importance of this meeting that Phillip had said would answer all her questions. The problem was, she didn't know what questions she had. He'd answered the most important one last summer—he had loved her mother.

ès

By ten o'clock everything was in readiness. Callie paced the wide balcony, listening for the sound of a car. Once she heard a motor, but it stopped at Grandma's. Unexpected company, she imagined, since Grandma hadn't mentioned anyone coming over this morning.

A few minutes later she heard the unmistakable sound of

a car making the laborious assent up Eagle Mountain. She ran into Morgan's study.

"He's on his way," she said breathlessly.

Morgan rose from his chair and walked with her to the living room. He put his hands on her shoulders and faced her. "This is going to be fine. You already know a lot of their history. This will just finalize it." He kissed her forehead.

When the doorbell rang, Callie answered it and stood open-mouthed as Grandma swept into the room in front of Phillip.

"Hello, Callie," Phillip said. "Since I promised you we'd talk about your mother, I thought Mrs. Duncan should be here, too. I hope you don't mind."

Actually, Callie was relieved. She'd known she would have to repeat to Grandma everything Phillip told her anyway; this would be easier. Callie glanced at Morgan who was shaking hands with her father.

"Welcome, P.J. Please come in and sit." Morgan had known P.J. as Dianne Prescott's much-older brother. They had never called him Phillip, or Morgan might have made the connection between the unknown Phillip who was Callie's father and P.J. Prescott.

"Grandma, why don't you sit right here." He motioned for her to sit in his recliner. He opted to sit beside Callie on the couch to give her his physical as well as moral support. But when he glanced at Grandma, he wondered if she might need him more.

She held her head in a straight upright position as if she were a mannequin in a chair. Her gaze stayed on Phillip. Morgan knew if this meeting was hard for Callie, it was doubly so for Grandma. Callie had never known her mother, Daisy but Daisy had been Grandma's only child.

Callie had met Phillip when he was in the hospital recovering from a car accident. When he was discharged, he had gone back to Boston, where he lived. They had talked on the phone, and he and his children had attended the wedding, but this was the first opportunity Callie had had for a face-to-face meeting.

The tension in the room was a palpable thing. Callie put her hand over her stomach, thinking this time she might really be sick from nerves. Grandma's posture was belligerent. Did Phillip have a chance of explaining his love for her mother?

"How have you been, P.J.?" Morgan said.

Phillip looked from Morgan to the women. "I think we'd better skip the small talk and get right down to why I'm here," he said. "I want to know my daughter better, and I know that won't happen until I've told all of you about Daisy and me."

He had sat in an overstuffed chair opposite the couch, but now he stood and walked over to glass wall and looked out toward Regal Mountain. "Twenty-five years ago my dad bought a house on Regal Mountain and I came to the mountains with my family for the summer. I was nineteen and had finished one year of college. I came to the mountains to figure out what I wanted to do with my life. My dad had been such a success as an inventor, and I felt I needed to succeed as well as he had. But I had no inclination toward engineering. I was much better at memorizing history dates than at plugging in numbers in a formula. I needed to declare a major in college, and I didn't know what to do. I needed time to think."

He motioned toward the view. "I hiked a lot that summer, on my own. That is, until one day in June when I was climbing this very mountain and saw the most beautiful girl in the world, sitting right here at the top."

Grandma gasped.

"That's right, Mrs. Duncan. It was Daisy. She was so bright-eyed, trusting, and innocent. We talked that day." He waved his hand as if correcting himself. "Actually, I talked and she listened. As we got to know each other, I listened to her dreams, too.

"We knew we couldn't see each other. My mother would have been displeased, to say the least, to find I was in love with a mountain girl. Mother has always been a social climber. When Dad bought the house on Regal, it was the beginning of her life as a socialite. And Daisy knew you wouldn't like her seeing a summer person, as you called us. She said you labeled us 'putting-on-airs people' and had no use for us."

For the first time Grandma took her gaze off Phillip and looked at the floor. Callie could only guess what was going through her mind.

"Daisy and I met here every day and then we started meeting at night between here and Regal. There's a path—"

"I've been on it," Callie said and knew that several times she and Morgan had followed the same path that Daisy and Phillip had taken.

"Daisy encouraged me to do what I wanted in life. Which I have. I majored in history, and I teach it at Boston University, but you know that. Our plan was for us to complete more schooling. Then I'd come back for her and we'd be married.

"I left with that understanding. However, Daisy never answered my letters, and I heard from her only once, indirectly. Mother said she had called and said she'd married a man named Sam. As you know, Mother intercepted Daisy's letters to me, and I believed her when she said Daisy had married someone else. There was no other explanation for why she didn't answer my letters. Of course, I now know she didn't get them. Mother took them out of the mailbox when I'd put them out to be picked up by the postman. So Daisy must have believed I didn't love her, just as I believed she didn't love me."

He walked back from the windows and plopped down in the chair, as if his tale had exhausted him.

"I never returned to the mountains until last summer. I stayed at school in the summers, and four years later married Louise. I thought I loved her at the time, but she never took the place of Daisy in my heart. We were married for eleven years she died. And we did have some good years together. You've met your half-brother and half-sisters." He looked at Callie as he spoke. "They'd like to know you better, too."

Callie swallowed hard and squeezed Morgan's hand.

Phillip reached into the pocket of his sports coat and withdrew an envelope. "These are the only pictures I have of Daisy. One evening we went into Highridge and played in the photo booth by the hotel. I had copies made for both of you." He handed pictures to Grandma and Callie.

There were four pictures with typical snaps of the two of them crammed in the booth. In two pictures they were clowning around, laughing. In one they were kissing. And in the last one they were looking at each other, love shining in their eyes.

"And now, I'd like to know what happened to Daisy." This time Phillip turned his gaze to Grandma.

She sat statue still, with tears flowing down her cheeks. She opened her mouth, then shook her head and looked at Callie.

Callie took a deep breath. "My mother wouldn't tell my

grandfather your name because she was afraid he'd hurt you. On the day I was born, the day she died, she called for Phillip over and over. That was all they knew of you."

Phillip bowed his head and cried.

eight

Callie closed her dry eyes and leaned against Morgan. What could she do for her grandmother and her father, these two who were hurting so? The picture of the mother she'd never met had touched her soul. She looked young, bright, happy, and so in love. But Daisy Duncan was only a picture to Callie. She wasn't a real person.

Grandma and Phillip had known this happy girl. They had both loved her. And Callie saw clearly that they both blamed themselves for her death.

"I should have been with her," Phillip moaned. He rocked back and forth holding his head in his hands.

Grandma still sat upright, mopping her tears with a hanky. After a long moment, she rose and walked over to Phillip and patted him on the shoulders. "There was nothing you could have done except love her. I should have let her see you. I didn't know. I suspected she had a thing for a summer boy, but I didn't want to know for certain. I was too scared of losin' her. And I lost her anyway."

Phillip stood and hugged Grandma. "I'm sorry," he choked. "But please understand that I loved her, too."

Grandma sniffed. "I can see that in the picture."

Callie turned to Morgan, still at a loss for what to do. He stood and pulled her up with him. "Part of Daisy still lives," he said and urged Callie to go to them.

"She has your green eyes," Grandma said to Phillip as she reached for Callie.

"But otherwise she looks like Daisy," Phillip said. "I'm

glad we have you, Callie." He pulled her into the circle, but turned his attention to Grandma. "Mrs. Duncan, forgive me."

"I do. Forgive me, too."

"Yes."

Now Callie couldn't hold back the tears. She broke away from her father and grandmother and reached for Morgan.

"Is now a good time for dinner?" Jean asked from the doorway.

"Perfect timing," Morgan said.

The mood of the group on the balcony was calm like a rainbow after the storm, Callie thought. God's promise to the world. There would always be an ache in Grandma and Phillip for Daisy, but the first offerings of peace had been extended and accepted. Callie hoped they could build on their shared love for Daisy, her mother.

Callie insisted that Jean join them for soup, shrimp salad, and fruit salad, feeling that another person might help with what might be a strained conversation. Then she offered a simple prayer. "Thank You, God, for bringing this family together and healing its wounds." The clanging of silverware brought a lighter conversational tone.

"Are you still eating beef stew?" Phillip asked. "I tried everything that could be beat to a liquid, and it was my favorite. But wouldn't you give anything for a thick steak?"

"I miss potato chips," Morgan answered. "Sometimes I get out the bag and smell them."

Phillip laughed. "Yeah, I remember. But it won't last forever. My wires came off in five weeks. Maybe you'll get yours off early, too."

Hope sprang in Morgan. "Just over two weeks and I could be okay?" he asked.

"Could be."

"Morgan's going to our doctor in town tomorrow, just for his weekly checkup," Callie said. "We've kept in touch by phone with his Atlanta doctor, but I don't think a trip back is necessary yet." She didn't want Morgan's hopes to be raised and then be plunged downward again if he had to wait the full six weeks.

Callie asked Phillip about his life in Boston and included Jean by talking about her search for a teaching job.

"Are you thinking of relocating or staying in the area?" Phillip asked Jean.

"Whatever's necessary. I like it here, but we could always come back summers."

What an odd turn of events, Callie thought. Here was Jean, who had lived here all her life, thinking of becoming a summer person. And Callie herself was now a summer person. Grandma's old adage about summer people and year-rounders not mixing was no longer applicable to their lives, if it ever had been. People were people, no matter where they lived at certain times of the year. Though unfortunately, there were those who were uppity, like Phillip's mother, Elizabeth.

She wondered what Phillip's relationship was with Elizabeth Prescott, but didn't get to ask until later that afternoon after Jean had delivered Grandma back down the mountain. Phillip and Callie went for a walk while Morgan lay down to rest.

"Things are very distant between my mother and me," Phillip said. "Once when I called to talk to Dad and she answered, I hung up. I wasn't proud of doing it, but something in me just slammed down that phone. I've spoken to her, but the last time I saw her was at your wedding. I need to talk to her like I've talked to Mrs. Duncan today. I need peace, Callie. I need to move on in my life. I regret a lot about my marriage to Louise, but I had three great kids with her, so there was good, too."

Callie walked arm in arm with her father and thought about the half-brother and half-sisters that she'd met, but didn't know. They lived in Boston, so getting to know them would not be easy, but perhaps when she could join them for a holiday sometime.

Again, she was becoming accustomed to money and what it could buy. All she had to do was call for a plane reservation and she could be anywhere in a matter of hours. When money wasn't an issue, overcoming obstacles was easier— if the obstacles weren't emotional problems of the heart.

Phillip left with the promise to return for another visit. Although they'd made great strides today, Callie wanted to know still more about her father.

Now that he was feeling stronger, Morgan prowled the house like a caged tiger. "I want to be normal again, get back to work. Do you think I could get these wires off in two weeks?" he asked. "Could we go to Atlanta to talk to the doctor? He'd be the one to take them off, wouldn't he?"

Callie glanced at her watch and saw she had just enough time to reach the office. Her call netted an appointment for the next day. Again, the power of celebrity and money spoke volumes.

"Do you want to spend the night? See Charlie and Harry?" If he met with them, perhaps she could sneak off for an appointment with her doctor.

"That'd be good," Morgan said. He went out on the deck and left Callie making phone calls to set up his meetings. First she called her doctor and confirmed that he would work her into his schedule Friday morning. At the same time, she set up meetings for Morgan and called Wilda to tell her they'd be returning the next day.

Jeff and the Richardsons were planning to come on Sat urday, but Callie would be back Friday afternoon in plenty of time to make last-minute arrangements for their visit She smiled as she remembered her last phone conversation with Jeff.

"Wait until I tell my friends I spent the weekend with Trey," he'd said, excitement coloring his voice. "They won' believe it."

Callie felt good that she could help this boy who had been through so much.

❧

At the crack of dawn on Thursday, Morgan was up and ready to go. Although Callie had told him there was no use in hurrying, since his appointment wasn't until one o'clock. he wanted to get back to Atlanta. He knew he'd get a good report from his doctor. Hadn't Dr. Doody in Highridge told him how quickly he was healing?

Oh, there were still yellow bruises, especially around his eyes, but that was minor. His chin had an angry looking scar, but that was going to be worked on. Maybe he could schedule that today. And what about getting those two front teeth? As soon as the wires came off, he wanted to be fit- ted for a bridge. Not that he minded the time in the moun- tains, but his time there this time wasn't a self-imposed exile, but a forced retreat.

When he couldn't make decisions for himself, he felt out of control, not a feeling he liked. He had always enjoyed doing for others, but he didn't like others doing for him. Again, the issue was control.

Because of Morgan's insistence on an early start, they reached Atlanta in time for morning rush-hour traffic. By the time Callie turned the van into the long driveway of heir home, her patience was worn thin, and she was glad or Wilda's welcome.

Yet, for the first time, Callie felt discontent in the Atlanta house. In the mountains she felt at peace. Here her houghts immediately went to the accident. Surely in time, hat feeling would go away.

Morgan also felt haunted by the accident. Odd, it hadn't bothered him to see the swimming pool before they had left for the mountains, but seeing it now brought back that night in pounding intensity. It would be three weeks tomorrow, but he felt half a lifetime had gone by since that filter had slammed into his face.

Wilda showed Morgan the mail that had accumulated. 'I was going to send another packet to the mountains today," she said. "This letter looked important."

Morgan studied the return address—the private investigator. He took the letter and a cup of coffee into his study. The pool man, Wayne Degraffenreid, was twenty-two and a high school dropout. He had found a day job just last week at a shoe factory. At night he played piano in an espresso bar. He'd worked a variety of jobs, mostly unskilled labor and always for minimum wage, and the location of his gigs had changed through the last five years, but he had always played music. He'd played with several bands. Sometimes he played keyboard instead of piano, but the hope was the same. Someday he'd get his big break and make records.

"Good news or bad?" Callie asked from the doorway.

Morgan explained the investigator's report. "It would take him forever to save enough money to pay the hospital bill. No high school diploma, but a love for music. I wonder if he's any good. I could put in a word for him as a studio musician."

"Could you use him?"

"No." Morgan chuckled in his closed-mouth way. "He plays piano—like me."

"Could we go hear him?"

Morgan lifted his eyebrows and that guarded look came back in his eyes to be replaced a moment later by a thoughtful expression.

"I could wear that fake beard and glasses. No one would recognize me. Why not? I've got plenty of strength now."

"You mean that beard you wore in the Christmas pageant in the mountains? It wasn't bad," she said. "Let's see what the doctor says. I should think an outing of an hour or so would do you good."

The doctor agreed that Morgan could do anything he felt he could handle. "But don't overdo," he cautioned Morgan. "We don't want any setbacks when you're doing so well."

"What about the wires?"

"The X-rays look good. I'll see you in two weeks and we'll make our decision then."

"What about the scar work?" Morgan asked. He wanted everything done now.

"We'll sand it, and it'll look much better. When the wires come off, we'll discuss it."

"Can't you do it now? Then when the wires come off it'll be healed, too?" Any delay only meant drawing out the time he couldn't be back to normal. "And my teeth?"

"Your dental work can start as soon as the wires are off. I suppose I could work on that scar. It's healed nicely, but I don't want to overload you."

"I can take it. Now?"

"Tomorrow morning, early. I can do it first thing . . . around seven or it'll be next week when I can get to it."

"I'll be here," Morgan said.

❧

The espresso bar looked like an old warehouse with a high ceiling and exposed heating ducts. The old wooden bar area, complete with bar stools, was in the center of the large room. Round tables dotted the space around it; at one end of the bar was a piano on a raised platform.

Morgan, disguised in his beard and dark glasses, and Callie sat as close to the piano as they could. At odd intervals noise from the espresso machine drowned out the sound of the piano.

Callie giggled and took a sip of her latte. "If this was the sixties, you'd fit right in," she told Morgan, "although you'd need a more colorful shirt, maybe with a rainbow on it. At this yuppie hangout, you stand out."

Morgan chuckled. He lifted his cup of cappuccino to her and carefully took a sip. He hoped no one could tell he couldn't open his mouth.

Wayne Degraffenreid sat at the piano and played old favorites. He swayed with the music as though feeling every note.

Someone requested "Autumn Leaves," one of Morgan's favorites for the piano. The trilling of the notes sounded like the leaves drifting from the trees to the ground.

Morgan leaned toward Callie so she could hear him. "He's good. Maybe I could get Harry to come listen to him."

"I like his sound. He enjoys his music," Callie said.

"He has a good ear."

They stayed for a few more songs, then Morgan escorted Callie to the car. "Why don't you let me drive?" he asked. "I know you don't like driving the van in city traffic."

"Not yet, Morgan. Didn't the doctor say you shouldn't

drive for six weeks?"

"But I'm strong again. I'm almost back to normal."

"I think it has more to do with the anesthetic and delaye
reflexes," she said. "Come on, think of it as being chau
feured."

He smiled and tried to think of it in her way, but this wa
one more area in which he felt out of control.

"How do you feel about helping Wayne Degraffenrei
when his carelessness caused the accident?" she asked a
ter they'd arrived back home. "I don't think I could be s
kind about it."

Morgan was silent for a long moment. "I'm not sur
how I feel. I wish it hadn't happened, but I know he didn
do it on purpose and that he is truly sorry for it. That doesn
excuse his actions, but I need to forgive him and forget i
If I can point him in the right direction in a career, it wi
help me make sense of all this."

"You're a good man, Morgan Perry Rutherford, th
Third," Callie said. "And I thank God every day that I'r
married to you."

"Words are cheap," he said with a teasing glint in hi
eyes. He put his arms around her and ushered her towar
the bedroom. "Show me."

nine

f Morgan had had any idea how much the sanding of his scar would hurt, he wouldn't have done it.

First the doctor gave him four shots in the chin and another above his lip. The physical pain was there, but the emotional pain was worse. The needles took him back in time to the night in the emergency room when he'd held the skin over his jawbone.

Then the doctor took an electric hand-held machine and sanded his skin. It was a disk of tiny metal razor blades. When it touched his skin, flesh and blood flew everywhere. What was left of his chin looked like a piece of bleeding raw meat.

Morgan didn't refuse the pain medicine the doctor gave him. Nor did he object when a ghostly white Callie took her place behind the wheel of the van.

"Why don't you lie down until Charlie gets here?" she suggested, and he went straight to the bedroom.

"I have some errands to run," she told him. "I'll wait until Charlie comes before I go."

How could she leave him when he felt so bad? His chin was on fire, he couldn't eat anything but watered down junk, and he needed her. And she was going to run errands? What was so important that Wilda couldn't do it?

When Charlie arrived, Morgan walked to his study and sat down heavily behind his desk. He heard the door shut behind Callie as she left.

"What happened?" Charlie asked, his eyes wide.

"This is plastic surgery. To remove the scar. Remind m‹ never to have a face lift," Morgan said without a hint o humor.

Charlie had brought lots of papers for Morgan to sigr some just letters, but he asked Morgan to sign them t‹ show the company was running on an even keel.

"I'll keep faxing you the day-to-day reports," Charli‹ said. "Everything's going smoothly. No strikes this sum mer." He referred to the threatened walkout by airline stew ardesses last summer. Morgan was glad he didn't have t‹ sit in on any labor negotiations. No union contracts ex pired this year.

Callie wasn't back by the time Charlie left, so Morgaı sipped a teaspoon of pain medicine. Now that the deaden ing shots had worn off, the pain was becoming intolerable

Another half an hour passed before Callie returned with out carrying any packages.

"How are you feeling?" she asked the moment she wa‹ back in the house.

He grunted a reply just as the phone rang.

Callie answered and immediately said, "What's wrong Marie? . . . I'm so sorry. Where is she? . . . Just a minute.

Callie turned to Morgan. "Marie's mother had a stroke Would you mind if I offer to take Jeff back with us? Theı she could devote her time to her mother and Jeff won't b‹ disappointed."

Morgan shrugged.

Callie took that as a yes and made arrangements witḥ Marie. "It's no trouble. We'll get a therapist in Highridge Don't you worry about it. We'll bring him back wheneve you need him."

Callie hung up and again turned to Morgan. "I arrange‹ to pick him up before three. That way we can get out o own before traffic picks up. Would you like me to get im, then come back for you?"

"Yes." He didn't want to meet the Richardsons looking ike he did.

"Harry's coming for lunch. Are you going to mention Wayne Degraffenreid to him?"

"No." He didn't feel one bit of charity toward the man who had caused this accident. Morgan closed his eyes to shut out Callie's questioning look. He didn't want her accusing him of going back on his word about helping that man. Had he actually said that helping Wayne would help him forgive him? He must have been affected by the man's music. Or was the effect of the pain on him making him so angry right now?

He lay down again until Harry arrived shortly before noon.

"Lunch is ready, honey," Callie called, and he forced himself to get up.

Lunch. Ha! His first course would be Instant Breakfast, chocolate flavored, followed by the ever-present beef stew. If he didn't take too long to sip those courses, he'd have time for ice cream before the others had finished dessert— but if he did take too long, then the others would sit watching him spoon each tiny morsel into his wired mouth. He was lucky he was missing his two front teeth so he had a hole through which to poke his food.

Feeling the drowsiness of the pain medicine, Morgan stumbled into the dining room.

"What happened to you, Trey?" Harry demanded.

"The doctor's working on his scar," Callie explained. "It should be healed in three or four weeks."

"Three or four weeks? What are we talking about all together? Another month or two before he's ready for the concert? Tomorrow's the first of June. That means the end of July or first of August before we can do it."

Morgan shook his head. The pain medicine was doing more than making him woozy. Now he was hearing things and seeing things. He saw Callie shoot Harry a warning look.

"What concert?" he mumbled.

Harry exchanged a secretive look with Callie.

"What concert?" he asked again. Something was going on and he wanted to know what. Had they been plotting behind his back?

Harry cleared his throat. "Have a seat, Trey." In an uncharacteristically mild manner, Harry said, "I know you prefer not to perform live anymore. However, that decision's been taken from us. Your fans need to see you in person on stage, singing like normal. Your career depends on it. They won't buy a studio shot or a video. We need the biggest concert of your life to show them that Trey's back."

Morgan was glad he was seated or he would have fallen over. "No way," he mumbled through his wires in his hoarse voice.

"Morgan, I believe Harry's right about this," Callie said, then turned to Harry. "Although now was not the time to discuss it."

Even she was against him.

"We don't even know if I can sing," he said.

"Of course you can sing," Harry said. "It'll take you a little while to get your voice back in shape, but we'll get you a voice coach. No problem. We have some details to work out. Where do you want the concert? New York? Los Angeles?"

"No concert," Morgan said.

"Trey, I appreciate how you must be feeling," Harry

tarted.

"No, you don't," Morgan muttered.

"I said this means your career, and I believe it. Fans ren't going to buy records if they think they're getting old ongs that we just hadn't released before. You need to be orking on new material, and you need to be seen. This ould be the biggest come back show ever. Barbra treisand, move over. Trey is back!"

Morgan closed his eyes and wished his manager was ack in his little office downtown.

"You can do this, Morgan. I know you can," Callie said.

"If you think it's so easy, you do it," Morgan said.

"I never said it was easy," she amended. "But I could do t, if I put my mind to it. Just like you can and will."

His chin had burst into flames; he knew it had. His mind vas cloudy with pain medicine that wasn't working ex-ept to dull his thought processes. And Callie was talking o him as if he were a little kid.

"I'll do it if you'll do it," he said.

Callie, her mouth hanging open, looked at him. Harry's yes were bugging out of his face.

"I'm not a singer," she finally said.

"You said you could do it if you wanted. Well, how bad lo you want it?"

"Morgan, you're tired, and I know you're in pain."

"Yes, I'm in pain. I've been tired for weeks. And I'm ick of this. Take it or leave it. Will you sing or not?"

Callie glanced at Harry, not knowing how to handle Mor-gan. She'd never seen him in a mood like this.

"Humor him," Harry said in a low voice.

"What?" Morgan demanded.

"Do you mean a duet?" Callie asked. "We'd sing to-gether?"

"Sure. A duet. Can you do it?"

Callie took a deep breath before she committed hersel
Of course, once Morgan was out of pain and was himsel
again, he'd renege on this agreement. This was pain talk
ing, that and the weeks of uncertainty that had dragged by

"Sure, I'll do it. I'll have to have a few lessons. Th
voice coach can help me, too."

"Shake on it," Morgan said.

Callie stuck out her hand, and he took it in his mucl
larger one. There was no gentleness in their touch, merel
a formalizing of a business agreement. Callie blinked bacl
tears and left the room.

⁂

As soon as Harry left, still growling as he walked out th
door, Morgan went in search of Callie, but she was no
where to be found. He wandered from their bedroom to th
spare bedrooms to Grandma's room before he asked Wild.
where she'd gone.

"She's getting Jeff Richardson. She said it would take ;
while to get him loaded. She'll be back for you by three."

He didn't feel like being polite to a stranger. Morga
didn't want to admit that he was jealous of an injured boy
but he needed Callie, and she seemed more concerned witl
Jeff.

In a moment of lucidity, he knew he was being ridicu
lous and unfair, but that moment was fleeting. He tool
more pain medicine, even though it wasn't time for an
other dose, and lay back down. He was asleep when Calli
came for him.

She hated to wake him up. If he felt half as bad as h
looked with that bloody face, then she could excuse hi
behavior today. She hoped he'd fall asleep once she go
him in the van.

She'd left Jeff in the van since she could hardly get him out on her own. Ken Richardson had lifted his son and belted him in a seat. Marie and Callie had wrestled the wheelchair into the van. Jeff had taken steps between parallel bars, but he couldn't walk on his own. The prognosis was good, but he had weeks of intensive physical therapy before he could graduate to crutches.

She was counting on Morgan helping her get Jeff out of the van. If Morgan wasn't feeling strong enough, and she'd been well aware of his staggering walk at lunch, then she'd call Phillip. She'd forgotten to call her father and tell him that she and Morgan were leaving the mountains for two days. He'd planned to spend time with her every day while he was in North Carolina.

Callie felt defeated. She'd been on a teeter-totter of emotions today. From the pain of seeing Morgan's face this morning to leaving him when he wanted her to stay. Seeing the obstetrician had given her new hope. With state-of-the-art Doptone equipment, she'd heard the baby's heartbeat for the first time through ultrasonic waves. But Morgan's reaction to Harry's concert ultimatum had reaffirmed her decision not to tell him about the baby until he had healed. He had too much to handle right now. Unneeded worry about her and the changes their lives would undergo with the addition to their family were concerns he could deal with after he was well. She had to protect him from those thoughts.

This wasn't a good day to bring Jeff back to the mountains. Morgan felt crummy and was acting worse, but knowing Jeff was in the mountains under the care of a therapist would take a load off her friend Marie. But how heavy a load could Callie handle?

She sat on the edge of the bed and touched Morgan's

hand. Somehow she'd get through this day, and tomorrow would be better.

"Dear God, please help us all work together and get through these trying times," she whispered.

Morgan opened his eyes. "I'm sorry," he said.

"I'm sorry, too," she said. "How are you feeling? Any better?"

"Still hurt. Time to go?"

"Yes. Jeff's waiting in the van." She helped Morgan get ready and said a quick goodbye to Wilda.

Jeff seemed thrilled to meet Morgan, and Callie could tell Morgan was trying his best to be kind to the teen-ager. Morgan explained that he was on pain medicine, and Jeff seemed to accept that explanation when Morgan fell asleep minutes after they left Atlanta. Callie used the drive time to chat with Jeff, enjoying the scenery and the peace that the mountains brought her.

With a much lighter heart, she pulled off the main highway onto the county road that led to Eagle Mountain. She stopped at Grandma's and introduced Jeff.

"Oh, Morgan," Grandma said when she saw him. Her expression showed her revulsion and pity. "Is it paining you?"

"Don't ask. My face is supposed to look better when it heals."

"It will. I reckon them doctors know what they're doing."

"I'll see you later," Callie said. "I need to get these guys home and fed. I've heard their stomachs rumbling over the motor." She put the van in low and started the hard pull up the mountain.

Phillip's car was in the driveway. What luck. Between him and Morgan, they could easily carry Jeff into the house.

Callie ran inside to get her father and found him and Jean in the kitchen. They hurried outside and a few minutes later had Jeff installed in his wheelchair on the balcony.

"What a view," he said. "This is fantastic!"

"Yes," Callie agreed. "I never grow tired of it. None of us do." She glanced around and was surprised to see Phillip and Jean standing close together and smiling at each other. Something was going on. It was in the air between them.

"I'm sorry I forgot to tell you we were going to Atlanta," Callie told her father.

"It worked out fine," Phillip said. "Uh, when I came over yesterday, Jean and I got to know each other better. Tonight we're taking in a movie."

Jean raised her eyebrows at Callie. "I hope you don't mind."

"Mind? Of course not," Callie said. "Enjoy."

❧

After a lasagna dinner that Jean had left for them, Morgan took more pain medicine and leaned back in the recliner. He'd helped Jeff into the bathroom and now that the boy shouldn't need anything for a while, Morgan could rest.

This might have been a mistake bringing Jeff to the mountains. He needed help getting in and out of his wheelchair, and he needed to exercise every day. Getting real exercise equipment and a therapist would have to wait until Monday. Meanwhile, Callie had asked Morgan to rig up an exercise bar outside tomorrow, and Phillip had said he'd help.

Morgan looked over at Callie and Grandma and Jeff playing dominoes at the game table. Jeff didn't have a chance of beating those two sharks, but he'd find that out for himself.

Jeff seemed like a nice enough boy. He had blond hair

and was tall, if his sitting height was any indication. His dark eyes held a sparkle that being in a wheelchair hadn't destroyed. Or had it been even brighter before?

He didn't seem to be in pain, or if he was he hid it well. Not like the pain Morgan was feeling. He hurt. He hurt on the outside, and he hurt on the inside.

How could Harry insist on a concert? And why did Callie agree with him? Because fans are fickle, a little voice inside told him, and he knew it was true.

After an accident like this, he had to make a public statement. He couldn't possibly answer all the cards that had come. He had to publicly thank his fans. And the only statement was a song. Center stage and personal—in front of thousands.

But why did the thought terrify him? God had always given him the strength to sing in spite of his stage fright. Wouldn't He help him now?

Morgan didn't know. He didn't even know if he could carry a tune. Would the hoarseness ever leave his voice? Why had God done this to him? Until he had an answer to that question, how could he sing?

ten

Morgan laid Jeff on the floor for his exercises.

"Marie gave me a list," Callie said.

"I know them," Jeff said. "Twenty-five lifts on each leg, then I do the elastic pull twenty-five times."

"Does it hurt?" Callie asked.

"No. Oh, a little," he revised his negative answer.

"Callie, I need more ointment put on," Morgan said. Horrible smelling stuff had to be put on his chin to keep the top skin from scabbing over and to let the bottom layer heal first. His face still looked like raw meat.

Callie glanced over at him. "Just a minute, honey." She handed the wide elastic band to Jeff, then she got the salve and gently touched Morgan's face.

"I'll put it on again around noon," she said. "How does it feel?"

"Better," he said. "Is it time for more medicine?"

"Not yet." She turned her attention back to Jeff. "How much weight do you put on the parallel bars when you're walking?"

"All of it," he answered with a grimace as he lifted his left leg a few inches off the ground.

"What could we use, Morgan?"

"I don't know," he said. That guarded look was back in his eyes, but she didn't know what to do about it. She could handle only one problem at a time.

"Could we use Grandma's sawhorses and nail a couple of long boards to them?" she asked.

"The runners should be round so he can grip them," Morgan said. "Long shovel handles from the hardware store might work. What time is Phillip coming? Maybe he could pick them up."

"That's a great idea. Why don't you call him while I help Jeff with the elastic pull?"

"You should take the van into town to get the handles," Morgan told Callie after he had spoken to her father. "Phillip doesn't think it would be safe sticking wood out his windows. He wants you to pick him up on Regal, and he'll go with you."

"Okay. Will you help Jeff while I go?" She smiled up at him.

"Sure," he said.

The minute Callie had left, Jeff said, "You're not like I expected."

"What did you expect?" Morgan asked.

"Someone bigger. Stronger."

Morgan drew himself up to his full height. "I'm six foot two," he said.

"Yeah, I know. I guess I meant bigger than life. I've seen you on videos."

That was common. Many fans thought of Trey as more than a simple mortal. Because his name was a household word, Trey was expected to live up to the image the press made for him. Well, he couldn't do that. He was just a man.

"You're just a guy who whines a lot."

Morgan took a step back.

"Callie, will you put some ointment on my face?" Jeff mimicked. "You should try being me and see how it feels to not be able to walk."

Morgan turned and walked out. This was not going to

work. When Callie got back with the wood, he'd tell her to take Jeff back to Atlanta.

"Morgan," Jean called a few minutes later. "Could you help Jeff into his chair?"

Morgan marched back into the den and glared at Jeff on the floor.

"Thanks," Jeff said.

"No problem," Morgan said shortly. He lifted the boy back into the wheelchair and pushed him out onto the deck. "Would you like a blanket?" he asked. "Early June mornings in the mountains aren't like the steam heat of Atlanta."

"I'm okay," Jeff said. "I like the cool."

"Fine. I have office hours. If you need something, call Jean." He was trying to be the adult here and be civil to the boy.

The twinkle in Jeff's eyes, which Morgan had mistaken last night for the sparkle of life, was pure mischief. Morgan pivoted and made for the sanctuary of his office. Catching Charlie in the office on a Saturday morning was a balm to his wounded ego. He had decisions to make. He was a person in charge. And he wasn't a whiner, no matter what Jeff thought. Was he?

When Callie returned with two extra long shovel handles and the sawhorses from Grandma's, Morgan had finished his call and helped Phillip unload the van.

"This should be fairly easy," Phillip said. "We can't drive a nail through these handles, but we can use nails as guides."

Morgan had no idea what he was talking about, so just held the handles in place while Phillip drove several nails on each side of them.

"How's he going to get inside this thing?" Morgan asked. Sawhorses at each end blocked access to the parallel bars.

"We'll have to lift him over, then help him turn around."

"It'll work," Callie said. "It's just a temporary measure. He won't be walking on his own for another six weeks, at the earliest. His physical therapist gets him upright every day. That's why I wanted this contraption."

"Let's get him to try it out," Phillip suggested. He disappeared into the house and returned pushing Jeff's wheelchair with Jean following behind.

"Morgan, give me a hand here," Phillip said. Together they got Jeff standing and lifted him over the bars so that by putting his weight on his arms and hands he could support himself.

"Can you put any weight on your feet?" Callie asked.

"I'll try," Jeff said.

In Morgan's opinion Jeff was playing the hero for Callie and Jean. Why couldn't they see through him? The kid felt as sorry for himself as Morgan did. Wait a minute, Morgan thought. He didn't feel sorry for himself. Did he? Did the others think he did?

He looked at Jean, but she wasn't watching him or Jeff. She had eyes only for Phillip. Just what he needed, a moonsick housekeeper. And Phillip stood beside her with his hand resting on her shoulder.

Morgan glanced at Callie to see how she was taking this. She'd finally accepted her father and her mother as a couple, as ill-fated lovers, and now Phillip was making a play for another woman. Okay, maybe he wasn't being fair to Phillip. Callie's mother had been dead for twenty-five years. A quarter of a century. Phillip had been a widower for ten. It was time for him to make a new life for himself. But Morgan didn't want Phillip's new life to hurt Callie.

"Thanks for making this exercise bar," Jeff said in a polite voice. He placed weight on his left foot and grimaced. In slow motion he moved his right foot in front of it, then the left, then the right.

"You're doing great!" Callie exclaimed. "Who knows what fresh mountain air and outside exercise will do for you."

Jeff sent her a doubtful glance. The kid wasn't as much a Pollyanna as he acted sometimes.

"Let's help him turn around," Phillip said.

Morgan took his place on one side of the makeshift parallel bars and lifted Jeff so that he could turn. At least, he thought, he was strong again. Oh, he got tired easily, but he could walk and lift things, and he was thankful for that.

After ten more minutes, Jeff declared he couldn't stand anymore, and the two men lifted him back into his chair.

Lunch was served in the dining room so that Jeff had plenty of room for his chair at the head of the table. Morgan sat on one side with Callie and sipped his soup. Jean and Phillip sat across from them.

"I called the office," Morgan said to make conversation. "Charlie was in catching up on what he missed yesterday. He's one dependable man. I don't know what I'd do without him."

Callie agreed. "What about Harry? Did you call him and work out the concert details?"

"No." Morgan didn't want to talk about the concert. He knew he had to do it, but he wasn't ready to work on it.

"You're doing a concert?" Jeff asked. "Can I go?"

"Probably not," Morgan said. "It'll be in New York or L.A."

Callie shot him a sharp look. "Actually the details haven't been worked out," she explained. "Harry would like a large audience. If you're walking by then, perhaps you could go with us." She smiled, then turned to Jean and said, "I was hoping your boys could come over tonight for a while.

Maybe play board games with Jeff."

"I'll ask them," she said. "Phillip was coming over for dinner to get to know them, but it might work better if we all came here."

"That would be perfect," Callie said. "Let's have a cook-out. Barbecued ribs, corn on the cob, potatoes in the coals." She cast an apologetic glance toward Morgan. "Would that be all right, honey? We could purée some meat for you."

Was this a social center? Morgan wanted a quiet night, just him and Callie, cuddled on the couch watching a movie on the VCR.

"That'll be fine," he said. He got up from the table and walked to the balcony. He couldn't refuse Callie the chance to spend time with her father. And he couldn't refuse her request to have the boys over for Jeff, but he felt as if he were being manipulated. Again his life was out of his own hands. He wanted control.

By six-thirty everyone was gathered around the picnic table, gnawing on corn cobs and ribs. Everyone, but Morgan. He stood by the brick barbecue grill and watched the others. Grandma had joined the festivities along with Ray and Brandon, Jean's sons. Before dinner the boys had played Frisbee with Jeff, making sure the disk was thrown straight at Jeff each time, so he could catch it. They were all getting along like a house afire, laughing and talking. Meanwhile, sitting at a dinner table and watching others eat was getting harder and harder for Morgan.

Grandma and Phillip were talking, both a little reservedly, but still they were communicating. Morgan thought their relationship had helped Callie more than her getting to know Phillip herself. But he didn't know. He and she hadn't talked about it.

How he loved Callie, and how he wished he had her alone.

He wanted to return to the days of April before any of this had happened. Maybe the two of them could go for a walk later tonight. A path led around the top of the mountain, dipping lower here and there, then climbing back up to the house. They'd enjoyed it in April, feeling so close to the moon and the stars and God.

God seemed to have deserted him now. He felt Callie drifting away from him, too. At times she was so preoccupied. Of course, there was her father. And he knew his accident had taken a toll on her. Now she had Jeff to think about, too.

Did whatever was going on between Phillip and Jean bother her? He hadn't had a chance to talk with her about it. Tonight they would. Surely the others wouldn't stay late.

His mind was clearer now that he hadn't taken any pain medicine since this morning. His face hurt less, and he'd put the salve on it himself, twice now. He toted the pan of leftover baked beans and joined the procession as the picnickers carried empty plates into the house.

"We'll have Grandma's homemade ice cream pretty soon," Callie announced. "I couldn't eat another bite right now."

The phone rang, and she grabbed it. After a moment, Morgan heard her invite Robert and Marilyn over for dessert.

"Robert finished the rough draft of his book," she said. "He's been a hermit since he came to the mountains," she explained to the others. "He's been too busy writing to socialize up until now."

When the newcomers arrived, the group settled down to a game of charades with one team against the other. Jean's sons and Jeff had never played the game, but they joined in with the exuberance of youth.

When ice cream was dished up, Morgan and Robert sat in a corner of the balcony.

"Well, what did your private detective come up with?" Robert asked. "Anything good?"

Morgan explained about hearing Wayne Degraffenreid at the espresso bar. "He's a good musician. I thought about putting in a good word for him with Harry. He might be able to hook him up with some studio work."

"But you haven't yet?"

"No, not yet. I didn't talk to Wayne. Callie and I went incognito. I wore a beard and glasses." Morgan stroked an imaginary beard.

"That was before you went for the rugged look, huh? That has to smart." He pointed at Morgan's chewed up chin.

"It hurts all right, but it's better now than yesterday. That was an all-time low. Now I just look like a piece of raw meat."

"Too bad I can't use that look in my book. Of course, a corpse wouldn't have a need for plastic surgery."

"So you really did kill a man off with my accident?"

"Worked like a charm—a carefully engineered feat of death. However, the bad guys were out to get Sinclair. Instead, they killed his friend. Morgan, this is the best book I've written. Now that I have the plot down, I have to fine-tune the murder and the consequences. But Sinclair isn't working for a client this time; he's working for himself and has a personal stake in the outcome. I've put more emotion in this one than any other book. Probably because I imagined you as the friend who took the hit."

"Glad I could be of use. Now I just wish this nightmare was over."

"Few more weeks, then you can talk and eat again?"

"Yes. And start dental work. Harry insists that I do a concert to prove to the world that I'm all right. He says my career depends on it. Callie agrees." He was asking a question without saying the words.

Robert rubbed his chin. "I suppose they're right. The sooner you do it, the more dramatic it will be. You don't want to do it?"

Morgan made a strangling sound through his wires. He didn't even know if he could sing.

"Well, old friend, I guess this is one of those times that separates the men from the boys. You'll do fine."

"Private conversation?" Callie asked from behind them.

"No," Robert said. "Just doing a little more work on my book."

"I thought you'd finished it."

"The rough draft. That's the quick part. The revisions take much longer."

"My accident worked as the murder," Morgan said. He handed Callie his empty bowl. "Good ice cream."

"Grandma makes the best," Callie said and smiled.

№

Morgan didn't get to talk to Callie that night. After their guests left and Morgan had helped Jeff to bed, he found Callie had already fallen asleep.

Morgan doctored the raw wounds on his face and slipped quietly in beside her. She murmured his name and turned over. He watched her sleeping peacefully. Her golden hair shone in the moonlight, and her steady breathing was a whisper of life to him.

He cherished this woman who had pledged her love to him, but he knew he hadn't shown it lately. Tomorrow would be different. They'd talk again like old times.

eleven

"I'm not going, Callie," Morgan said. "I'll help you load Jeff, but there will be plenty of help at church to get him out."

"Why won't you go?" Callie asked. Her face had clouded over, and he hated seeing that look in her eyes.

"Look at me. I'd scare half the people there."

"You went last week. They didn't care what you looked like. Didn't you notice that?"

"They were very nice. But this week I look worse. Please, Callie, I'd rather stay alone."

"Oh," she said in a small voice, and he knew he'd hurt her. She'd misinterpreted what he meant. Or maybe she hadn't.

A few minutes later he lifted Jeff into the van and folded the wheelchair and stowed it behind the seats. As soon as Callie started the slow descent of the mountain, Morgan set out for a walk.

He'd wanted Callie with him, but he needed to commune with nature. To find God again. He'd done a lot of thinking last night as he lay in the dark with Callie asleep beside him. In the quiet, pain had returned, and the deepest pain of all, the sense that he'd been deserted by God, came back to him now, clear and sharp.

Many times he'd asked why this had happened to him. He'd given surface answers, like helping Callie know Phillip, but that would have happened without the accident. That Phillip came to the mountains now was a direct result of Morgan's retreat to heal, but father and daughter would have rendezvoused in the mountains sometime this summer anyway.

Certainly Robert would have come up with another idea for a book without Morgan's getting hurt. Robert never had a shortage of ideas in his mind. Morgan had always accused him of being the one who hatched the plots that had gotten them in trouble as youngsters.

There was the matter of the pool man, but Morgan hadn't made up his mind about helping Wayne Degraffenreid get work in the music field. Perhaps his talent would be discovered without any interference from Morgan.

So, what was the reason Morgan had been injured? Did God have some divine plan for him that he couldn't see? Or had God turned his back on Morgan P. Rutherford, the Third?

He walked from the house to the opposite side of Eagle Mountain and sat on a huge rock that jutted out, forming a precipice. From his vantage point, he could see miles and miles. Regal Mountain wasn't far from here as the crow flew. Although fully leafed trees hid most of the houses, he could make out a rooftop here and there.

A robin sang a song from a tree behind him. Other birds answered his call. Here, high above the rest of the world, Morgan found a little peace.

The rhythm of the wind as it tossed the tree limbs back and forth made a natural sound that God had ordained. If there was order to the world, and God had created that order, then why had He allowed Morgan to be hurt? And when would this ordeal be over and life return to normal? Was there a lesson to be learned from this? If so, what was it?

Morgan stared at the sky above the peaks of the Blue Ridge Mountains and the far distant peaks of the Great Smokies. Was there a prettier place in the world? He doubted it. He was one of those summer people that Grandma had distrusted, but he felt as if his heart belonged in these mountains where Callie's roots were and where their future would be.

The Atlanta house was in another dimension, another time and space where corporate decisions were made. This place was Morgan and Callie's home. This land inspired him.

With a purpose to his step, he followed the path back to the house. For the first time in over three weeks, he sat down at the grand piano in the living room and played "Amazing Grace." It was the first song that came to mind, probably because he sang it at every concert. It was his closing song.

Now it was his beginning. If he was going to sing in public again, and in a big way if Harry had anything to do with it, he needed some new material.

He pulled out blank sheet music from the piano bench and penciled in notes and words as they came to him. This was going to be his finest concert. If he could sing again. But he pushed that negative thought from his mind.

Callie heard the music as soon as she entered the house, and her heart was gladdened. She'd wondered how long Morgan would take to get back to what he loved best.

She walked up behind him and put her arms around him. "Solitude must have done you some good," she said and kissed him on the neck.

He pulled her around until she was sitting on his lap. His kiss was still tentative. In two weeks he would be able to kiss her in the old way with no wires to hamper him.

"Jeff's in the van," she said.

"Okay," he said in his hoarse voice. He kissed her once more, then walked hand in hand with her to the door.

Grandma sat in the van with Jeff. She gave Morgan the

straightforward searching look that she was famous for, then nodded. "Feeling better?" she asked.

Morgan nodded and turned his attention to setting up the wheelchair and getting Jeff into it.

Callie and Grandma got busy in the kitchen while Morgan wheeled Jeff out to the balcony, where the boy normally sat. Morgan sat in the porch swing and pushed himself off with his foot.

"We got off to a bad start yesterday," he said. "I'm sorry I was so short with you. But I'm not a whiner. You met me at my worst time."

Jeff eyed him suspiciously, but when Morgan walked over to him with his hand outstretched, he shook it.

"New start?"

"New start," Jeff said.

"So, how was church?"

"Small, but there were two or three cute girls there."

Morgan smiled. Jeff was a normal seventeen-year-old boy. Why hadn't he looked at him as a boy/man who needed help instead of lashing out at him as he had yesterday?

"That Darlene's something, isn't she?"

"Yeah. She's a good-looking girl and nice, too. She have a boyfriend?"

"I don't know. You ought to ask Callie. The girls confide in her. Did they talk to you?"

"Yeah. They asked me how it happened and all."

"You know, I don't know how it happened. Callie mentioned a drunk driver."

"Head on. The guy hit me not two blocks from my house. I was lucky he wasn't going any faster or he could have creamed me. I'd been to a baseball game and had dropped a friend off at his house, so I was alone.

"I couldn't believe it when his headlights came at me. I

honked my horn, but they just kept coming straight at me." Jeff's voice rose as he recounted the events of that night.

"I thought he'd veer to the right, but he never did. I go as far over as I could. I guess that's why he hit my side so hard. It's like it happened in slow motion."

"I know what you mean." Morgan told the story of his accident and the way he'd seen the filter lid fly at him "Was the other driver hurt?" he asked.

"Broke his arm. That's all. I hope it was the arm he used to lift his beer to his mouth. Maybe it will keep him off the streets for a while. It was his third time to be picked for driving under the influence."

"I'm surprised he had a license."

"He didn't. It was suspended, but that didn't stop him He goes to trial the last part of June. This time I hope they throw the book at him." Jeff's tone had gotten louder and louder. "The guy's got money and power. If it's possible he'll beat the charge." He looked down at his legs. "I don' know why this happened to me instead of him," he said vehemently. "Why am I the only one to suffer? I have to work and work to get back to normal. And he has a cast on his arm. It's not fair."

Morgan was silent for a moment. This boy was going through the same thing he was. "Seems like there should be a reason, doesn't there? There *should* be a lesson learned by that man or by you or by someone. Some good should come out of this."

"But what?" Jeff raised his hands up, acknowledging he had no answer.

"Dinner's on," Callie called from inside the house.

Morgan pushed Jeff inside and stopped the wheelchair at the head of the table. Today he didn't feel the animosity he had yesterday at Jeff's taking his traditional seat. He gave the boy a smile, then bowed his head to ask the blessing.

"Dear God. Thank You for this day and this food You have given us." He paused and glanced at Jeff, then closed his eyes again. "We need Your help today. We need to know why our accidents happened. Is there a reason? Are You teaching us something? Please show us why. Amen."

"Amen," Grandma said. "So, you two want to know why? I've asked that question a lot in my life, and there's not always an answer we see. We have to accept what happens and go on."

Callie glanced from Morgan to Jeff. Were they getting along now? Yesterday's animosities hadn't escaped her, even though both males had tried to cover their feelings. She'd prayed they could help each other through their trials, and God seemed to have answered her prayer already.

"What possible good could come out of your accident?" Callie asked Jeff.

"Nothing."

"Oh, think about it. Could this serve as an example to other teens? Could they understand the importance of not drinking and driving? Could they see what happens? Could they learn how to drive defensively? Not that there was a thing you could have done differently. By pulling over and slowing down, you may have saved your life."

"And how am I going to be an example? Who do I tell?" asked Jeff.

"Seems to me there was a big wreck with a singer some time back. One of the Mandrells," Grandma said.

"Barbara," Morgan said. "She posed for a poster promoting the use of safety belts after she and her kids were hit head on. She said the belts saved their lives."

"Well, then you do the same," Grandma said.

Jeff waved his fork at her. "Who would listen to me? I'm

no big star." He pointed his fork at Morgan.

They were all looking at him. "Hey, I'm not going public with a face like this."

"Maybe you wouldn't have to show your face," Callie said. "What if you and Jeff did an interview with a magazine. The reporter could take pictures of the back of your head and Jeff in his wheelchair. I'll bet Harry would jump on the idea."

"We want to reach teen-agers, not music fans."

"If one person, no matter what age, listens and learns, then you've got a reason to go through this." Callie motioned to the wheelchair.

"What about Robert?" Grandma asked. "He might know a writer for a teen-agers' magazine."

"Robert wrote for magazines before he sold a novel. He might be interested," Morgan said.

"Would you call him? Please?" Jeff asked.

"Can't hurt to ask," Morgan said, getting caught up in the enthusiasm. Maybe some good *could* come out of Jeff's being hurt.

&

Later that afternoon Robert came over.

"I haven't written for magazines for over ten years, but I don't think I've lost my touch. I'll have my agent market an article, offering only one-time rights, so we can hit as many magazines as possible. Let's make a list."

He had brought along an old market book that listed magazines and their addresses.

"Most of the teen magazines are aimed at Sunday school audiences," Callie said as she flipped through the pages.

"You want to hit those, too," Grandma said. "Even Christian kids with good values go astray now and then. You've got to warn everybody."

"Grandma has a point," Robert said. "We'll let my agent worry about the markets. Let's get to work on the article. We'll need pictures of you and Morgan out on the exercise bar. I could get a photographer from the Highridge paper to come out and snap a few thirty-fives. Tell me everything you remember about the wreck, and I'll work something up tonight. Then tomorrow we'll get the pictures."

As she listened to Jeff's story, Callie wiped away tears. She already knew the story, but she was so emotional these days, the result, she knew, of all the extra hormones coursing through her blood.

"Jeff is only telling you half the story," she said. "The other half is from his parents' point of view. Marie and Ken have been through so much with this. While Jeff was unconscious, they didn't know if he would live or die. The parents' story is one that should be told, too."

"I have to work Trey into it, too," Robert said. "Using your influence is how we'll get this into print."

"Having a famous mystery author write the story isn't bad, either," Morgan said. "Editors would have to be nuts not to go for this story."

The next afternoon Robert brought a photographer with him and set up the photo shoots.

"Careful to get Morgan in the shots, but keep his face in shadow," Robert directed. "We want to see these pictures tomorrow." He had interviewed Marie and Ken via phone and had his agent making calls. "There's nothing new about this story. It's repeated over and over every day. But my agent says with Trey involved, it's a story magazines will buy. I'm going to mention that you two were in the hospital at the same time. That's the connection—recuperating together. I'll touch briefly on your injury, Morgan, but not take the focus off drunken driving."

The following day, Morgan, Jeff, Robert, and the photographer were poring over photographs.

"This one on the exercise bar is excellent," Morgan said.

"Yes, but we'll use this one of you lifting Jeff over the side rail to get him standing up. Shows teamwork," Robert said.

Morgan looked at Jeff whose eyes were sparkling again. He had insisted on doing double time on the exercise bar that day. Jeff wanted to walk, and he wanted it now.

Morgan wanted to be well, too, but there was nothing he could do to help himself. No amount of exercise would help him get the wires off any quicker. But the excitement of the article made him make a decision about Wayne Degraffenreid.

He called Harry.

"All I want is your opinion. Listen to him play and see if you think he could be a studio musician. If you don't want to take him on as a client, that's your business." Morgan also told him about Jeff's article, and Harry was all ears.

"We need a headline in the tabloids, too. That'll hit the stands a lot quicker than magazines with a big lead time. Everybody reads the front pages in the checkout lines. The in-depth stuff can come later."

"Whatever you think," Morgan said.

"I'm going to leak some information on a come back concert," Harry told him. "Know where you want to do it?"

Morgan noticed that his agent took it for granted that he would be singing. "New York."

"Central Park? Yankee Stadium?"

"You work out the details. That's your job. I'm writing new songs."

"Best news I've heard all day," Harry said. "Look for your name in the papers."

twelve

Callie was sick again. She'd hoped that last week's episode would be the one and only, but a few days later she woke up early and knew if she moved, she'd throw up.

With iron determination, she slipped out from under the sheet, covered her mouth with her hand, and ran noiselessly down the hall to a guest bathroom. She sank to the floor beside the toilet and emptied her stomach.

"Callie?"

She should have known. He slept so lightly these days. Morgan got her a wet washcloth and helped her to her feet.

"I think I ate too many sautéed mushrooms last night. Or maybe it was the butter. Sometimes I react to too much butter." The excuse was the best she could think of. "I think in this case you're lucky you aren't eating solid food yet," she tried to joke.

"Are you all right? Ready to get back to bed?" He led her back down the hall. "Why didn't you go to our bathroom?"

"I didn't want to wake you."

"Callie, I'm here for you. Don't ever worry about waking me up if you're ill. Now, how about some ginger ale and crackers?" Again, he relied on the only remedy he knew.

"Okay, thanks." She rested with a cloth on her forehead until Morgan returned.

"Just a sip, then you have to eat a cracker," he instructed, just as he had a week earlier. "I don't like seeing you like this, Callie. We've got to make you well."

"I'm all right."

He sat on the bed next to her. "I've been wondering how you feel about Jean and Phillip."

"I think they deserve each other. They both can make their own happiness, but they'd be better off together. Did you think it would bother me?"

"I didn't know. Since you're just getting to know him as a father, to throw in Jean, too, seemed a bit much."

Callie shifted on the pillow, and Morgan lay down beside her and slipped his arm around her. "He will never be a father to me. Not like . . . well, since I've never had one, I'm not sure what I'm saying, but not like your father was to you. Didn't he teach you right and wrong, and play baseball with you? Didn't he hug you and love you?"

"My father was the best. He did all the things a father should do. He was a good provider, but he made time for his kids. Vic and I had our private line to his office. No matter what meeting he was in, if we called, we were to be put through immediately. I remember once I called when he was having a board meeting, much like the one I missed a couple of weeks ago. Mom had said I couldn't go skating with some friends, and I wanted a second opinion. He said I should never question my mother's decisions. And I didn't get to go skating for two weeks."

"You'd make a good father," Callie said.

Morgan raised his eyebrows. They had discussed this before, but he wasn't willing to risk Callie's health to have a child. She had told him that Daisy's death from childbirth wasn't due to a genetic defect, but he also knew that Grandma had had four stillborn babies. He wasn't going to put himself or Callie through anything so traumatic. Maybe they would adopt.

"Thanks," he said and switched the topic. "How about

another sip?" He held the glass of ginger ale for her and handed her another cracker.

Callie was sick once more before she was able to crawl out of bed and into the shower. Then she felt normal again.

Jean eyed her suspiciously when she appeared in the living room. Callie averted her gaze. Grandma knew, she felt sure that Jean knew, and she didn't want to talk about it until she could tell Morgan.

"Could we talk a minute, Callie?" Jean asked.

Here it comes, Callie thought. "Of course. Is this a private conversation?" she asked and waved toward the den where Morgan and Jeff were playing chess.

"For now," Jean said. "Join me in the kitchen?"

Callie watched Jean make hamburger patties for tonight's cookout when her sons were coming over again to see Jeff. The sight of raw meat made Callie clutch her stomach. She sat on a bar stool and turned toward the window.

"It's about your father," Jean said. Callie felt relieved, but didn't answer. She couldn't face that meat again. "Uh," continued Jean, "I know we've known each other only a week, but we've been seeing each other a great deal. Not just the time he spends over here, but in the evenings, too."

"Yes, I know," Callie said.

"I think I love him," Jean said softly. "I know it's soon after my husband died, but my feelings for Phillip don't diminish my feelings for David. It's like two different parts of my life."

Jean walked behind Callie, forcing her to turn around. With the intention of reassuring Jean that she was glad she had found love, Callie gasped instead as her eyes fell on the hamburger patty Jean was holding in her hand. Callie ran for the bathroom.

A few minutes later, Callie returned to the kitchen. "Jean,

I'm sorry. I was sick this morning. I think too much butter last night. Sometimes it affects me that way. I'm delighted you and Phillip have found each other."

From Jean's look, Callie didn't think she believed her excuse about the butter, but she didn't know what else to say unless she told her the truth about her illness. What a tangled web, she thought, remembering the old adage about lies. Even little ones told to help others grew and grew until they ended up hurting others anyway.

"I'm sorry," she blurted. "It wasn't the butter. I'm pregnant."

"Ah," Jean said as if that made sense of everything. "The raw hamburger?"

"Yes. I haven't told Morgan because he needs to concentrate on himself, not me. Please don't tell anyone, not even Phillip. I want Morgan to be the next to know."

"I thought it upset you that Phillip and I were getting close."

"I know or I wouldn't have told you my secret. Promise me."

"Oh, I promise I won't tell, but it's not something you can keep a secret for long. Have you seen a doctor?"

"Both here and in Atlanta. I'm healthy and taking vitamins," she said as Jean ushered her to a chair. "And I'm not an invalid."

Jean laughed. "My natural instinct is to protect a pregnant woman."

"That's one reason I'm not telling Morgan yet. When the wires come off and his face is healed, he'll be able to concentrate on my pregnancy better."

"You're probably wise. His moods swing even more than yours . . . and I remember what pregnancy does to your emotions. Did you realize he and Jeff were at war for a while?"

"I knew they resented each other."

"I heard them Saturday when they didn't know I was around. I'm glad they've made peace. Wonder what did it?"

"Prayer changes things," Callie said. "And I prayed mighty hard about it. So did Grandma. God knows I needed them to help each other."

Morgan poked his head into the kitchen. "Are you feeling all right?" he asked.

"I'm fine."

"Do you feel like running an errand into town? We need to get a walker for Jeff."

"Do you think he can use a walker already?"

"No, but the physical therapist thinks it would be an incentive. He could stand up in it in the house and get in more exercise than with the bars in the yard."

The therapist hadn't been able to come on Monday when Callie had called, but she'd come out Tuesday morning and had already been here today. Callie had talked to Jeff's mom and assured her Jeff was doing his exercises. Since Marie's mother was still in the hospital, she agreed that Jeff could stay in the mountains until she could care for him again.

"I'm on my way," Callie said to Morgan. "Do you want to ride along?" Morgan's only trips to town had been to the back door of the doctor's office.

"No," he said quickly. "I'm headed for my office."

Grandma went to town with Callie, and they hit the grocery store as well as the library. They stopped at the bank and had coffee with Joe. He accepted an invitation to the cookout. Why not turn it into a real celebration? Callie wondered. She wasn't sure what she was celebrating, but she had a new life in her, Jeff and Morgan were friends now, and Morgan was playing the piano again. The old Morgan wasn't back yet, though. This Morgan was still subject to high and low swings instead of the even balance of the old Morgan. But he was on a high now, and she wanted to capitalize on it.

≈

Back on Eagle Mountain, Callie called Marilyn and Robert and invited them, too. As soon as she hung up the phone, it rang.

"Callie, my folks are here," Phillip announced without preamble. "I thought they were coming up next week after I left, but they decided to come early."

"I see," Callie said, but she didn't see what Phillip wanted from her.

"Would you like them to come to the cookout tonight? I've talked to Mother, and she's apologized for lying about Daisy and keeping her letters from me." A long moment passed. "I'd like them to meet Jean." Another long moment. "Callie? Are you ready to make peace with them?"

No, she wanted to scream. "Please bring them," she said instead.

Callie ran for Morgan's study. "Cooper and Elizabeth Prescott are coming tonight," she said. Morgan stood and reached for her, and she flung herself at him and hugged him close. When she looked up at him, though, all she could see was his raw chin. It hadn't bothered her before, but now it reminded her of raw hamburger and that thought sent her running to the bathroom.

Morgan followed her and got the cold washcloth as he had earlier. "You've got to settle this thing with Phillip's family," he said. "I hate to see you tearing yourself apart like this."

Once Callie was lying on the bed, with her gaze averted from Morgan's face, he paced back and forth.

"If you don't want them here, I'll call and tell Phillip not to bring them," he said. "But you have to face it sometime. You said you felt better about Phillip and your mother after you talked with him and Grandma. Do you think it would be the same if you talked to the Prescotts in the same way? Not tonight with the others around, but now. Or this afternoon."

"She hates me," Callie said, and Morgan didn't have to ask who "she" was. Elizabeth Prescott had made no secret of her dislike of Callie when she'd learned about her granddaughter. Only after hearing that Callie was engaged to Trey had she changed her attitude, and that fit with what Phillip had told them of her social climbing ways.

"You can't let someone else have control over your emotions," Morgan said. "If you hate her back, you're giving her power over you . . . and you're using energy in a negative way." He sat down beside her, but Callie still wouldn't look at him.

"I admit I didn't feel charitable toward the pool man who put the wrong size of bolt on that filter. Now that I've worked through it a bit, I feel better, though. Harry should have gone to hear him play last night."

"I didn't know you'd told Harry," Callie said. Why were they keeping things from each other? In the past they had shared everything.

"I called him yesterday, but I guess I forgot to mention it to you," Morgan said. That eased her mind somewhat. At least he hadn't intentionally not told her information. "Now, back to Elizabeth Prescott. What do you want to do?"

To know Phillip better meant understanding his family. But she didn't want to see Elizabeth. She'd rather be stung by a hundred wasps, but she recognized that this was not something she could avoid. Better to get it over with and move on. Elizabeth's rejection had lurked in the back of her mind for too long. "I want to see her this afternoon."

"Good. Do you want me to go with you?"

"Yes. Do you mind?"

He leaned down and kissed her. Callie closed her eyes so she wouldn't see his face.

"Callie Duncan Rutherford. I am your husband, and I will always be here for you. Just like you've been here for me through the accident." He kissed her again, then reached for the phone.

❧

Later that day, Callie said to Elizabeth, "I wanted to see you this afternoon to get rid of bad feelings between us."

The older woman, carefully made up and with every dyed chestnut hair in place, sat in a wing chair in the great room of the Prescott home on Regal Mountain. Cooper, her husband and Callie's new-found grandfather, shared the couch with Phillip. Morgan and Callie sat together on the matching love seat.

"Phillip and I have been through this," Mrs. Prescott said with a lift of her chin. "I believe that was sufficient. It's a family affair."

"But I'm family," Callie said.

"Yes, Mother. Callie is my daughter." Phillip turned to Callie. "I understand that what Mother did, she did thinking it was the best thing for me. However misguided her motives, she was thinking about me. I accept that. Now she must see how her decision affected others."

For the first time Mrs. Prescott looked directly at Callie. "I suppose you want me to say I'm sorry."

"I want you to say what you feel," Callie answered. "I'm

sure it's hard knowing you have an illegitimate granddaughter. It was hard for me to accept that myself. I thought I was an orphan, and believe me that was easier to take. Until last summer, I didn't know my father was alive. But now I'm delighted to know him." She smiled at Phillip. "And I know he loved my mother."

"They were too young to know what love is," Mrs. Prescott said. "They would have ruined their lives."

"Did you know my mother?"

"No. But I could tell from her letters that she wasn't who I had in mind for Phillip. I wanted him to be happy."

"And you were the judge of his happiness?"

"You don't know what it's like to be a mother. When you have children and are concerned about their marrying the right type of person, then you'll understand."

Callie sat rigid. Didn't she already feel protective of her unborn child? Would she be as interfering a mother as Elizabeth Prescott? No, she would not. She would remember how lives could be destroyed or changed forever as a result of one person's choices. She would teach her child right and wrong and pray that her child made correct decisions. And she would respect her child's choices. Phillip was nineteen when he had met her mother. That was young, but it wasn't the same as a fifteen-year-old boy having a crush. Still, she could see that a mother might have a hard time realizing when her child was mature enough to make wise decisions.

She didn't want to understand Mrs. Prescott's actions, but now, in spite of herself, she found she did. But could she forgive her? She would try.

"Thank you for sharing that," Callie said. "I understand your actions, although I don't agree with them." She stood and said goodbye. She shook hands with Cooper Prescott and then held out her hand to Mrs. Prescott, who finally reached for it with a limp handshake.

❧

"That wasn't exactly a meeting of the minds, but it may be all you ever get out of her," Morgan said as Callie drove them back to Eagle Mountain. "She's a cold woman."

"Yes, but I feel better for going over there. Do you think they will come tonight?"

Callie had her answer when Mrs. Prescott sent her regrets with her husband.

"Elizabeth has developed one of her headaches," Cooper said. "But I wouldn't miss this cookout for the world."

thirteen

During the following week, Callie's nerves were on edge. She experienced no more morning sickness, but she dreaded waking up in the mornings, not knowing if she'd feel sick or how to cover it up if she was.

Morgan worked on songs, but as the date neared for the return to Atlanta and the wires to come off, he was short-tempered. When he voiced his doubts that he'd ever sing again, Callie would reassure him, and that seemed to help for a little while. Then she could tell from his attitude that his doubts had returned.

Meanwhile, Callie watched Jeff struggle with pain, exercising his legs until he neared exhaustion. His parents had agreed he could stay until Morgan returned to Atlanta to have his wires removed. Jeff vowed he'd walk off that van when he returned home.

Phillip came over every afternoon to visit and left with Jean when her workday was over. Mrs. Prescott did not call or send any messages via her son. Callie truly didn't care. She had found a measure of peace in herself by understanding the woman's motives. She had forgiven her, although she didn't care if she ever saw the woman again.

Grandma watched Callie like a hawk and fussed at her about nutrition. "You're eating for two now, Callie Sue. You make sure you give my great-grandchild a good start in life."

On Wednesday Jean fidgeted as she worked around the house at the top of Eagle Mountain. "I got a contract to teach in Highridge next year," she told Callie. "Fifth grade. What do I do? Sign it and obligate myself for an entire year or wait until Phillip says something?"

"What do you expect him to say?"

Jean laughed, a self-conscious sound. "The big four words: Will you marry me? Why would he when we've known each other only two weeks and he leaves on Friday?" She plopped down on the couch in the living room and burst into tears. "What should I do?"

Callie put her arms around Jean and cried tears of empathy. Her father was leaving, and they were now friends. They'd talked about Callie's going to Boston to visit with Phillip and his kids, her half-brother and half-sisters, but they hadn't finalized anything. Not that she should cry about that, but she cried at anything these days.

"What's wrong?" Morgan asked from the doorway. He crossed the room in quick strides and pulled Callie into his arms. "Are you hurt?"

"We're okay," Callie said and took the handkerchief Morgan offered her and mopped at the tears that wouldn't stop. "Jean got a teaching job."

"Congratulations, Jean. So these are tears of happiness?"

"No. She wants to marry Phillip," Callie said and sobbed.

Morgan's eyebrows shot up. "Does he know that?"

"Of course not," Callie said. "She can't tell him."

"Why not?"

"Morgan, you don't understand," Jean said. "This job in Highridge is an answer to prayer, but now I want to go to Boston."

"What's wrong?" Jeff wheeled himself into the living room.

"Nothing," Morgan said. "It's too complicated for mere males to comprehend."

"Not funny, Morgan," Callie said. "This is serious."

"Then Jean had better talk to Phillip, but we don't need to interfere."

"Morgan, I can't just call Phillip and tell him I want to marry him. I have responsibilities, two sons to raise. That's a lot to ask a man to take on," Jean said.

"True," Morgan said, "but how else will he know? Give him a chance. The worst he can say is 'no.' "

"Someone's coming," Jeff said and wheeled himself over to look out the east wall of windows. The sound of a motor, chugging up the mountain got louder and louder.

A few moments later a florist truck pulled up to the house. All four of them watched as the delivery man carried a giant bouquet of roses to the door. "Flowers for Jean Garvey," he said.

With shaky hands Jean took the roses and carried them to the dining room table.

"Let me guess," Morgan said as Jean picked the card out of the bouquet and read it. She placed her hand over her heart.

"Phillip wants to take me to dinner tonight. Just the two of us."

"All right!" Callie exclaimed. "This is your golden opportunity. Go call him and accept. What will you wear?"

"This is out of our league," Morgan said to Jeff. "Ready for exercises on the bar?"

The two males left for outside, and Jean made the call. She came back into the kitchen with her face glowing.

"We're going to Collett's. Fancy. This must mean something."

"Of course it does," Callie assured her. "You must leave here early so you have plenty of time to get ready." The phone rang, and she said, "I'll get that."

The superintendent of the Sunday school had talked to several members of the small congregation who wanted to have a surprise party for Morgan. "He was so good to raise all that money for our church last summer. Now that he's hurting, we want to do something for him. Do you think he'd come to the church tomorrow night or should we come to him?"

Morgan had refused to go to Sunday school for the second Sunday in a row. His face looked much better now. It no longer had the raw meat look, but had scabbed over and looked like a giant strawberry that baseball players sometimes get when they slide into home.

"I can get him to Grandma's if you could hold it there." That way Morgan could claim tiredness and retreat to the top of the mountain if he wanted. She had no idea if a party would cheer him up or not.

They arranged the covered dish dinner and music party. Callie immediately called Grandma, who had already talked to several people about the party. "This here's a perfect place," she said. "We're having us a music party. Think that'll make him happy?"

"I don't know, Grandma. He's up one minute and down the next. He wants so desperately to sing, and he's afraid. We'll know more Friday when the wires come off. This can't be a late party, because we'll head to Atlanta by six the next morning."

Callie almost asked if Jean and Phillip and Marilyn and Robert could come, but decided against it. Although Grandma had come a long way toward accepting summer people as regular folks, others in their church were uncomfortable around the wealthy summer crowd. This was a church picnic, and she guessed it should stay that way.

Callie wound up her talk as Morgan came in pushing

Jeff in front of him.

"Grandma wants us to come to dinner tomorrow night. Around six. Is that all right?"

"Sounds fine. Jeff's going to walk now. Want to see?"

Callie followed them to the hallway that led to the bedrooms. Morgan set the walker exactly in the center between the walls and wheeled Jeff to it. "Careful to balance before you move it," Morgan said as he helped Jeff stand. Callie pulled the wheelchair a few feet back.

Jeff clutched the walker as he had been doing all week. He'd stood for as much as fifteen minutes in the past, although his arms had borne most of his weight. This time he started as he'd practiced. He took a deep breath and lifted the walker. Before he could set it back down and move his feet, he tumbled face forward and landed in a crumbled heap on top of the tipped-over walker.

"Are you all right?" Callie exclaimed.

"I'm okay," he said. "I thought I could do it." Frustration made his voice rise in pitch.

Morgan helped him up. "You pushed your hands to the center before you lifted the walker. You have to lift it from the side to keep your balance. Now, let's try again."

Callie scooted by them and repositioned the walker. She stood in front of it and held it in place as Jeff took his place.

"Okay, move out, Callie. I'm ready."

"Can I hold it in place, so you won't go down again?"

"No. I'm going to do it by myself."

Callie stepped back and watched the determined teenager. He gritted his teeth and painstakingly moved the walker forward a few inches. His left foot took a step followed by his right.

"I did it!" he exclaimed, his face brightening with joy.

"Again," Morgan said calmly.

Jeff repeated the slow process four more times. "That's enough for now," Morgan said. "We'll try it again in an hour." He moved the wheelchair behind Jeff and helped him sit.

"Didn't your therapist in Atlanta say there was no way you could walk for at least six weeks?" Callie asked. "If she thought you could make this much headway so quickly, I doubt she'd have okayed your coming to the mountains without her supervision."

Jeff's grin stretched from ear to ear. "Won't she be surprised? Wait until Mom and Dad see me."

"They'll be thrilled," Callie said. She leaned over and hugged the boy. "I knew the mountain air would do you good. This is a healing place. We're high in the air, closer to God." She glanced at Morgan and hoped he'd agree, but he merely nodded.

When his Highridge therapist arrived, Jeff showed off his new skill. The rest of the day Jeff practiced with the walker for ten minutes at the stroke of the hour. He fell three more times, but only, he stated, because he got overconfident and didn't take his time. By nightfall Callie was exhausted by his efforts and didn't know how he could even stand up to try again. He went to bed early with the promise of starting the regime again the next day. "We can take Grandma's sawhorses back to her tomorrow when we go to dinner," he said as Morgan helped him get into bed.

≈

By eight o'clock the next morning, Jeff had already had his first walking session. He and Morgan sat on the balcony. With the sound of Jean's car climbing the mountain, Callie rushed out the kitchen door, waiting impatiently for the news.

"Well?" she said as soon as Jean stepped out of the car.

"It didn't come up," she said.

"You didn't ask him how he felt?" Although Callie understood why Jean couldn't say anything, she knew the clock was ticking away the minutes until her father would be leaving for Boston.

"I thought he'd say something. We had a wonderful time, and I told him about the teaching contract." She shut the car door.

"What did he say about it? That should have made him make a move," Callie said as they walked into the house.

"I thought so, too, but he said he was glad I'd gotten what I'd wanted."

"Well, don't sign that contract until he's gone."

"That's tomorrow, Callie."

"But you never know the difference a day can make. Just think, if you two married, you'd be my stepmother, wouldn't you?"

"I guess in a way, I would," Jean said wistfully. "I'm going to make something special for Morgan, since we hope this is his last day to eat puréed food. Has he already eaten?"

"He's had an Instant Breakfast, but he's always hungry." Callie took her cue from Jean and turned to a different subject.

Later that morning she talked to Phillip and arranged for the two of them to go into Highridge for tea. It would be their last time together since he was leaving the next day for Boston at about the same time that Callie was leaving for Atlanta. "I'll pick you up," she told him. She wanted to check with Grandma and see if she could get any supplies for the picnic while she was in town.

"Everybody's bringing their own table service," Grandma

said when Callie suggested she pick up paper plates. "I'll take care of you and Morgan and Jeff, so Morgan won't suspect anything."

"What about balloons? Can I supply those? That would lend a festive air. We could tie them to the poles on the front porch."

"Good idea," Grandma said. "Balloons are good."

Callie left Grandma's house and drove straight to Regal Mountain. Phillip was sitting in the yard waiting for her, so she didn't have to go up to the Prescott house. She wondered if he had done that so she wouldn't run into Elizabeth Prescott. Callie really didn't care anymore, but she imagined he would take a while to realize that. He seemed subdued on the curvy ride into town.

When they were seated on the open-air balcony of the Highridge House overlooking Main Street, Callie brought up the subject of Jean. Morgan had said she shouldn't get involved, but she hated seeing two people she loved so unhappy. And unless she missed her guess, Phillip's mood was directly related to Jean.

"She's going to teach next year. That's what she wanted. She told me she was praying for a contract when we first went out," Phillip said.

"Maybe that's what she wanted before she got to know you," Callie said as nonchalantly as she could, then took a big bite out of a cookie.

"Do you know something I don't know?"

She chewed slowly and swallowed the cookie while she studied his face. "I doubt it. Of course, you know she loves you."

With a bang, Phillip set his glass of lemonade down on the table.

"She loves me? She didn't tell me."

"Of course not. Did you tell her that you loved her?"

"No. I didn't want to cloud the issue. She got the contract she wanted that lets her stay in the mountains. I knew she wouldn't want to leave."

"Men! Why can't you read minds?" Callie said and looked up at the ceiling.

"What should I do?"

Heeding Morgan's warning not to interfere, although she already had, Callie said, "That's between you and Jean, but I think you should be honest with each other." She saw him glance at his watch. "Are you ready to go? I need to pick up some balloons."

Phillip helped her stuff the car with helium-filled balloons, allowing only enough extra room for the two of them. "Would you mind helping me unload these and tying them on Grandma's porch? I can take you home after I check on Morgan," Callie said, hoping that Jean would be driving Phillip home.

He consented and, from the look in his eyes, Callie figured he knew the way her mind worked. Maybe there was something special to this father/daughter thing.

At the top of the mountain Callie climbed out of the van and invited Phillip inside. They'd left Grandma's porch looking like a carnival booth.

"I'll just be a minute," she said. "I want to make sure Morgan doesn't need anything."

Phillip followed her into the house and into the kitchen where Jean was whipping up a pudding treat for Morgan.

"Could we go for a walk?" Phillip asked.

Jean glanced at Callie, who looked as innocent as she could manage. "Go on," Callie said. "I'll finish this." As they walked outside, Callie poured the instant pudding into a bowl and carried it to Morgan.

He was in his study, just hanging up the phone.

"Harry," he told her. "He's heard Wayne Degraffenreid play several times now and took George Warner to the coffee shop, too. Wayne has a short-term contract to go on the road for two months while George's keyboard man is home on leave. The keyboard man's wife is having a baby in a week or two, and he's taking off to be with her now and after the baby's born."

When he mentioned the word "baby," Callie unconsciously put her hand to her stomach. Realizing what she had done, she quickly removed it and clapped her hands. "That's great news, Morgan." George Warner wasn't a giant name in the business yet, but he would be. For now he was the opening act for other singers. This job was bound to lead to others for Wayne Degraffenreid.

"Yes. It's another good thing to come out of this accident. Pudding for me?" He nodded toward the bowl Callie still held.

She handed it to him. "Uh, Jean fixed it special for you. She and Phillip are on a walk."

Morgan raised his eyebrows. "Do I smell a meddler?"

"Not really. I just told him they should be honest with each other."

"Honest? As in, you love her and she loves you, so why don't you do something about it?"

"Now, honey," Callie said. She walked around the desk and sat down on his lap. "Love is something to celebrate. It's not something to miss just because you misinterpreted the other person's actions. Take this action." She kissed him tenderly on his lips. "How would you interpret that?"

"I need another sampling before I can make a clear decision," Morgan said.

She kissed him again. "And now?"

"Callie!" Jean shouted from the hallway. "Where are ou?"

In her haste to get off Morgan's lap, Callie nearly fell. We're in the study," Callie called. Oh, no. Jean sounded s if she were boiling mad. Had Callie done the wrong hing telling Phillip how Jean felt? In her mind, Callie re-,ressed to fifth grade when she'd told a boy that her best ,irlfriend liked him. Morgan had been right. She should ever have meddled.

"Callie," Jean called again. She appeared in the door-vay with Phillip on her heels, her face glowing, her eyes lancing. "I quit," she said. "I'm getting married."

fourteen

"Wow! I mean congratulations." Callie hugged Jean and then Phillip. Morgan shook hands with her father.

"When's the happy event?" he asked.

"The boys and I are going to visit Phillip in Boston in a couple of weeks. As soon as I can get things worked out," Jean said. "Then we'll set a date. Phillip thinks it's only fair the boys see what life will be like in the Northeast. We can come back to the mountains for summers. Phillip won't be teaching every summer session like he is this one."

So, another year-rounder would become a summer person.

"And you're walking out on the job, are you?" Callie asked. "Good thing we're headed back to Atlanta tomorrow."

"I could come back for another week, if you need me," Jean offered.

"No need. Now that Morgan's strong again, I can handle things," Callie said.

"You mean Jean was a babysitter?" Morgan asked.

Callie opened her mouth, then closed it. The others laughed, and even Morgan smiled as much as his wires would allow.

"Now why couldn't I see through this situation before?" Morgan asked.

"You've had a lot on your mind," Jean said. "Callie didn't want to add to it by making you aware you needed someone with you."

The two couples walked back to the kitchen. Jean told Jeff her news and said goodbye. "I know you'll be walking in no time."

"We're going to Regal to tell my parents," Phillip said, "then we're going to talk to Jean's sons."

"I'm so happy for you," Callie said and kissed her father goodbye. "Have a safe trip tomorrow."

"You, too. I'll be calling you, Callie, to arrange for a visit." He hugged her and whispered, "Thanks for telling me to be honest today," then he let her go and climbed in the passenger seat of Jean's car.

"Call when you get back to the mountains. If you need me, I'll come help," Jean said.

"I'll call, whether I need help or not," Callie said.

She and Morgan waved goodbye as Jean backed the car around and headed down the mountain.

"Well, since you brought those two together, I guess you're all right with it?" Morgan asked. "It doesn't bother you that your father is getting married again?"

"No. I hope he is happier this time. He deserves a new start in life."

"An example of the prodigal son?" Morgan asked.

"Yes, in a way. Yes."

૨&

Callie and Morgan walked back inside in time for Jeff's hourly ordeal with the walker.

"Can I take the walker to Grandma's tonight?" he asked.

"I don't see why not," Morgan said. "You can show her your stuff."

When it came time to go to the foot of the mountain for the surprise party, Callie loaded Jeff's wheelchair into the van. She wanted him to be mobile with all the others around. He could show them his walking progress, but she didn't want him in danger.

Morgan was looking backward as he talked with Jeff, so he didn't see the cars at the foot of the mountain when they came into view.

"Morgan, close your eyes," Callie said. "Grandma wanted your last night on puréed food to be special, and I helped her decorate for her dinner. I don't want to spoil her surprise."

"Close them now?" he asked, although she could see that he'd already followed her request.

"Yes. We put balloo . . . Wait, I'm not telling what we did. Just keep those eyes closed tight. I'm not much good at keeping secrets from you," she said, although she'd done an outstanding job at keeping the biggest secret of her life.

"Jeff, watch him. Don't let him peek." Callie winked at Jeff, who knew all about the surprise.

Jeff laughed. His mood, which had climbed higher with every step he took, was contagious.

Callie maneuvered the van close to the porch. Other vehicles were parked up and down the lane from the highway. The crowd of about thirty people stood around the porch and waited in silence for Callie to come around to Morgan's side. First she opened the sliding door, so Jeff could be part of the surprise, then she opened Morgan's door.

"Keep them closed until I say you can open them," Callie instructed. "Watch your step. Okay, now open."

"Surprise! Surprise!" the group yelled in unison.

If it could have, his mouth would have dropped open. As it was, Morgan's eyes widened and he raised his hands up as if to say, "How did you manage this?"

Grandma stepped off the porch and hugged Morgan. "We want to send you off to Atlanta in a big way," she said.

'When you come back, we know we'll have a hard time keeping you quiet."

"This is wonderful," Morgan said, although he knew that not many of them could hear him. He said it again, as loud as he could, and church members shushed each other.

"I'm deeply touched by this party. I didn't have any idea. Callie said I had to close my eyes because of some decorations." He motioned to the balloons that adorned the spindly porch columns of the old farmhouse. "How could you all be so quiet? Did you hold your breath?"

The crowd laughed.

A fiddler struck up a tune and the group launched into "For He's a Jolly Good Fellow." A couple of other musicians with guitars jumped in. When the song ended, the crowd cheered.

The superintendent of the Sunday school stepped forward. "You were here for us when we needed our church repaired. Now we're here for you since you need to be repaired. So, let's pray before we dig into this delicious food."

Members bowed their heads and the old man continued. "Lord, we want to thank You for this and every day You give us. Bless this food for the nourishment of our bodies and bless those who prepared it. And help this fine man find inner peace and let him sing for our enjoyment again. Amen."

"Amen" resounded through the group before several conversations started at once.

"Morgan, you get to lead us through the line," Grandma said. "Point to anything you think can go in the blender, and I'll mush it up. Callie, you fix a plate for Jeff." Someone had helped Jeff into his wheelchair and had pushed him to a spot not far from where the musicians had drawn up chairs.

Callie followed Morgan through the line. He settled for the chicken and noodles that had become a staple in his diet and took a piece of lemon meringue pie for dessert. He couldn't eat the crust, but he could slowly manage the filling.

The Sunday school superintendent sat down beside Morgan on the porch. "We've missed you the last couple of Sundays." It wasn't an accusation, just a statement of fact.

"I looked so bad, I didn't want to scare the congregation," Morgan said.

"They wouldn't have been scared. You might have found some answers."

"To what questions?" Morgan asked. He wasn't sure where this conversation was going.

"What questions do you have?" The old man asked a question of his own.

Morgan sighed. "Several. The biggest question is why did God do this to me?"

The screen door slammed behind Grandma as she came out of the house. "Here you go, Morgan." She handed him the same bland-looking puréed gunk he'd been eating for five weeks.

"Thanks," he said and stirred the thick liquid. Would he really get to eat solid food tomorrow?

Grandma moved back to the food line, and the old man picked up the conversation where it had left off.

"God didn't do this to you. As I understand it some young man made the wrong decision about a bolt on a filter. The filter clogged because of dirt and the pressure blew the top off. You can't blame God for this. We all make choices, be they right or wrong. God knows which one we're going to make, but He lets us choose."

Morgan looked into the old man's clear gray eyes. He had seen so much in his eighty-some years. Surely experience had given him this wisdom to see what Morgan couldn't see.

"So, accidents happen," he said.

"Yes, as a result of our choices. What has happened to the young man who chose the wrong bolt? Have you forgiven him for making the wrong choice?"

"The man's a nighttime musician. I asked my agent to listen to him play and maybe hook him up with a job that he'd know how to do."

The old man smiled. "Did he get a job?"

"Yes. Just today."

"You're a good man, Morgan."

"No. I didn't want to help him. I could have called my agent a couple of weeks before I did."

"But you did call. That's what matters. God didn't make the decision for you. He gave you time, and you did the right thing. I'm sure He approves." The man stood up. "I've got to get in line or all of Grandma's fried chicken will be gone."

Morgan stared after the old man. He thought his name was Mr. Burch. He'd have to ask Callie, because the old man had made more sense out of this accident than anyone else had. It was an accident, plain and simple. Accidents happened because of people's carelessness or ignorance or both. God didn't have it in for Morgan. He had let others make choices.

"Our choices affect many people," Morgan told Callie, when she sat down beside him on the porch.

"Yes, they do," she said. "And we try to make good ones."

"We try. But we don't always. Is that Mr. Burch?" He pointed to the old man.

"Yes. He's been superintendent of the Sunday school for almost thirty years. He's never abused the power, so he's reelected time and again."

"He told me that God didn't cause this accident. People's choices caused it."

Callie put down her plate and looked at Morgan. "I know. Do you remember our conversation in Atlanta? I told you I caused the accident or I contributed to it by placing that plant too close to the edge of the pool, so when it blew over, it went into the water."

"But you couldn't have known the wind would come up."

"No. I didn't know. But I made the choice to set that plant stand where I did. If I had set it back another three feet, the filter wouldn't have clogged." Callie sniffed. They had been through this before, but obviously the issue wasn't settled.

"It would have clogged another time and blown, and you might have been injured. That would have been worse."

"I would have rather it had been me," Callie said.

In spite of the others around them, Morgan kissed Callie. "I'm glad it was me. Now, enough of this. We're at a party to celebrate my wires coming off. Let's eat." He lifted up his bowl of gruel as a toast.

As soon as all had eaten and covers had been put on the leftovers, the musicians tuned up, and the folks sang in an old-fashioned hootenanny. Morgan hummed along. He had worked at saying clear, full sentences in conversations, but he didn't struggle with the words of the songs.

Tomorrow. It couldn't come soon enough.

The party broke up around ten, and Morgan loaded Jeff into the van. Amid cheers, he'd shown the church members his walking ability.

"I can't wait until tomorrow," Jeff said as the van climbed Eagle Mountain. "Mom and Dad aren't going to believe this." Morgan knew exactly how he was feeling.

✿

They left even earlier than they'd planned. Morgan was awake by five, and Callie didn't think that Jeff had slept at all. Both males shifted nervously in their van seats, a feat that Jeff hadn't been able to do just two weeks earlier.

"I told Grandma that Phillip and Jean were getting married," Callie said. "She took it okay. She likes Jean, too."

"Good," Morgan said.

"Good," Jeff said.

"I told the man in the moon that we'd fly up there for dinner," she said.

"Good," Morgan said.

"Good," Jeff said.

"All right, guys, I'm through talking, since you're not listening. Let's listen to music."

"Good," Morgan said.

"Good," Jeff said.

Callie found a station and drove the rest of the way humming along by herself as the two nervous males fidgeted.

First stop in Atlanta was Jeff's house. His parents were out the door before Callie shut off the motor.

Ken opened the side door and Marie climbed in the van and hugged her son. "I've missed you so much," she said. "Did you have a good time? Did you do your exercises?"

"Every day," Jeff said. "How's Grandma Hinkley?"

"She's much better," Marie answered.

"Hey, would you and Dad get my wheelchair out of the back?" Jeff asked nonchalantly.

His parents went to the back of the van and pulled the wheelchair out. While they were out of sight, Callie set up the walker on the driveway, and Morgan lifted Jeff out of the van.

"I won't be needing that," Jeff said as his parents wheeled the chair to the side of the van. He took a few tentative steps.

Callie grinned at the expression on the Richardsons' faces. "He's not real mobile yet, but he's been walking for a couple of days now."

"I can't believe it," Ken said. "This is impossible. You weren't to be walking for a few more weeks, if then."

"Good mountain air and a positive attitude got this boy on his feet," Morgan said.

"We can't thank you enough," Marie said.

"We didn't do it," Callie said. "He did."

After walking a bit more, Jeff allowed himself to be carried into the house since there wasn't a ramp for the wheelchair. He submitted to the chair again, but not for long, he assured them. He was going to continue his every-hour walking routine until he didn't need the walker anymore.

Callie and Morgan stayed for coffee, and Morgan took a pill the doctor had prescribed he take before the wire removal procedure. They left the Richardsons with promises to return in a few days.

"Next stop, wire removal. Are you ready?" she asked as she drove them to the doctor's office.

Morgan took a deep breath. He felt more out of control than he ever had. The pill had taken effect, and he could barely keep his eyes open.

He was taken right into the office and the doctor came at him with shot after shot. Just as the last time he was in the office, he experienced déjà vu. He relived the night of the accident, and the emotional scars within him bled, revealing themselves in tears that stained his cheeks.

Callie held his hand as the doctor used pliers to untwist he wires and pull and tug and jerk them out. He gripped er hand as if it were a lifeline, squeezing hard. It was her ifeline, too, as the room spun and she fainted and sank to he floor.

fifteen

Through the pain, Morgan knew Callie had gone down, and he called to her in a muffled voice. The doctor's hands were still in his mouth, but Morgan shoved them away with his free hand. His left hand still held Callie's. In his drug-induced stupor, Morgan crawled off the high examination table and crouched down beside her.

"Get a wet cloth," the doctor ordered, but the nurse already had one on Callie's forehead and another at the back of her neck.

"Callie, can you hear me?" Morgan asked. He could barely talk. One loosened wire dug into his tongue.

She moaned.

"Honey, wake up. Wake up."

She was out for only a moment, but it was a lifetime to Morgan. If anything ever happened to Callie, he didn't know what he'd do. She meant everything to him.

She fluttered her lashes, as if it was too great an effort to open her eyes.

"Callie."

This time she opened them and took a shallow breath and then another.

"What happened?" she asked in a small voice.

"You fainted. Did I squeeze your hand too hard?"

She lifted her hand to wave his question away, but it was too heavy to keep in the air, and she let it fall down to her side. Her head ached.

"Let's get her up on the table," the doctor said. Although

Morgan had been drugged, his mind was now crystal sharp, and he lifted her and placed her on the examining bed. He took a chair beside her.

"Are you all right?"

"I feel weak, but I'm okay. Sorry. This whole thing got to me."

"Nurse, stay with her," the doctor said. "I've got to get these wires out while he's still somewhat numb."

"No. I'm okay." Callie sat up on the table and motioned for Morgan to take her place.

"Honey, you'd better lie back down."

She shook her head. "I'm okay. Let's get this finished and get home."

She sat in the chair Morgan vacated and again held his hand as the doctor wrestled the wires out of his mouth. Morgan didn't squeeze her hand this time, although she knew the pain had intensified as the pain killer wore off.

When it was over, Morgan and Callie took a cab home. "Neither one of us should be driving now," he had told Callie. "We'll send someone back for the van."

After returning a call to his mother, Morgan lay down and insisted Callie join him. "I know you were frightened for me, but you're still looking pale. And I need you with me."

Callie needed the rest. She'd had an early morning filled with anticipation and pain. But she slept as fitfully as Morgan, who felt as if he'd been in a fight and come out the loser. His face ached and his mouth was full of the metallic taste of blood.

Dorothy and Victoria delivered the van and were waiting to see them when they got up a couple of hours later.

"Oh, Morgan, how do you feel?" his mother asked. "Your chin is healing. Can you talk?"

"I can open my mouth all right, and I'm hungry for something that I can chew. Problem is," he said with a lisp, "I need my two front teeth." His voice was as hoarse as ever.

"Morgan sees a dentist on Monday," Callie said. "In a couple of weeks he should look much better." She felt rested now and ready to cope with Morgan's pain again.

Although he didn't mention how he felt, the frown lines on his forehead had deepened, and she saw pain in his eyes.

"What about the concert you mentioned last week when we talked?" Victoria asked. "Have you scheduled it, and are you giving us tickets?"

"Always after a free ride, Vic," Morgan teased, but the frown line remained etched on his forehead. "I don't know when it is, but we've decided on New York.

"Where the Blue Ridge meets the Smokies," he sang, "Lies the place that I love best." He was actually singing, but the hoarseness wouldn't go away. "Where the deep sky meets the mountain peaks and the tall trees give—"

He stopped when his voice cracked and he looked with fearful eyes at Callie.

"It'll take a while to get back in the swing," she said. "Maybe we should look into that voice coach."

He nodded. "I'll take some lessons with you. Get my voice back in shape."

"Callie, you're taking lessons?" Dorothy asked.

"No, well . . . ."

"Callie's singing a duet with me at the concert," Morgan announced.

She had thought he'd forgotten about that promise that was made when he'd been in such pain from the plastic surgery. Surely he wasn't going to hold her to it.

"It was one of the conditions of my doing this concert. I'm writing a special song for us." He crossed over to the piano and sat down. He'd thought of letting Callie out of the deal, aware that she'd agreed to it only to get him out of the doldrums and back into his old life again. But at times lately she'd seemed so distant. He'd catch her with a faraway look on her face, and when he'd asked about her thoughts, she'd said she just had a blank mind. He didn't buy that. Something was bothering her, and he couldn't break through the barrier that she'd thrown up between them. Practicing together, a situation that brought down a person's defenses, might help her open up to him. He didn't want secrets between them. He loved her with all his heart and wanted them to always be close.

He played the melody with one finger, all he could manage in his current state of mind and body.

"Sounds lovely. This should be a real treat to your fans. After 'Callie's Song' won video of the year, they want to see more of her, don't they?" Victoria asked.

"Yes. She's definitely the better half of this whole," Morgan said. "A lot of the cards and letters we've gotten are giving *her* support because I'm hurt." He understood that. He would've needed support, too, if their roles had been reversed.

Dorothy and Victoria stayed for lunch and seemed to enjoy watching Morgan eat solid food as much as Callie did.

"Any more chips?" Morgan asked. He could chew fine with his back teeth. His front bottom teeth felt odd, but then, they had no top teeth to match up with.

He took a bite of a ham and Swiss cheese sandwich, not his choice in what his first meal should be, but Wilda had explained she didn't know exactly what he'd be able to handle. He wasn't tasting much anyway, since his mouth and tongue were still stinging.

"Fried chicken for supper?" Morgan asked and the house-keeper promised to fix the special meal.

"Mashed potatoes and gravy?" she asked.

"No. More potato chips," he said and took a handful from the bowl she had refilled.

❧

Dorothy and Victoria left shortly after lunch, and Morgan lay down again. As soon as she was sure he was asleep, Callie called her doctor and told him about fainting.

"I'm sure you're fine, but if you want to come in, we'll listen to the baby's heart to make sure."

Callie lost no time in driving to the office, where the nurse ushered her in and hooked her to the listening device. The heartbeat was loud, and Callie breathed a sigh of relief.

"Are you taking your vitamins?" the nurse asked, and Callie assured her that she was. Fainting that morning had been a fluke. Seeing Morgan's anguish was more than she could handle. She felt certain it wouldn't happen again.

She left with a lighter heart, but with another decision confirmed in her mind. She'd planned on telling Morgan about the baby today, but she'd wait until he was better. His concern for her in the doctor's office reaffirmed her thought that he needed to concentrate on himself and not on her health. She'd see how the visit to the dentist's office went on Monday. Then she could tell him.

❧

On Monday, Morgan was more than ready for his trip to the dentist, a place that from childhood had given him a stomach-tightening feeling. Each time he looked in the mirror and stared at the unsightly hole in the front of his mouth, he more desperately wanted teeth. His bottom ones didn't feel right, either, and he had given them a pretty good working out, eating everything he'd been craving for five weeks.

Callie seemed more secretive. He hoped his imagination was working overtime, but he felt she was keeping something from him. He set up a voice lesson for Tuesday, and had the voice coach come to the house. Singing in front of a critical audience might make her open up. He knew his attempt at psychology probably wouldn't measure up to any scientific approach, but it was the best he could do.

The dentist took molds for his front teeth, promising a new permanent bridge within ten days. He put temporary teeth in place, but they were yellow and too big.

"Your bottom teeth are dead," the dentist told him. "That's why they haven't felt right to you. We'll start root canals on Wednesday."

"He could have said we're putting you in front of a firing squad, and I'd have been more relieved," Morgan told Callie on the way home. "I wish I could get over my fear of the dentist's chair." On the positive side, he was behind the wheel for the first time since the accident, and he felt good to be in control again instead of being a passenger.

That's what he had been for the last five weeks—a passenger in life. Finally he was taking control again, bit by bit.

He headed for the office as soon as he took Callie home. Now that he could open his mouth without a black hole, he felt he could face his employees. He wasn't ready for his fans yet, though. They expected a bigger-than-life persona. He wasn't there, yet.

As soon as Callie got into the house, she called Grandma. "I've waited too long. Every time I set a time to tell him, something else comes up and I delay. Now it's gone too far. I don't know how to tell him about the baby."

Grandma chuckled. "If you don't tell him soon, he'll notice

on his own. You can put it off another month, but is that fair to Morgan? Callie Sue, you've got to tell him tonight."

But she didn't. He was full of office talk. Even though he had been on top of the business via the phone, that wasn't the same as being there in person to read expressions on faces. He was going back tomorrow after their morning voice lesson.

That thought paralyzed Callie. How could she go through with a duet? At least he didn't expect her to sing alone.

❧

At ten the next morning, Callie sang scales for her new voice coach.

"She has good pitch," Annette Hamilton told Morgan, as if Callie weren't in the room. "She could be very good."

For the next hour, Callie practiced singing from her diaphragm. Morgan's lesson was less intense, since his hoarseness continued.

"What did the doctor say about your vocal chord?" Annette asked.

"In another week or so it should be reconnected to the cartilage," Callie explained. "Then the hoarseness should disappear." She knew Morgan had hoped he'd speak normally when the wires came off, but they were still playing the waiting game.

Morgan went to work, leaving Callie to practice on her own. She sang as she went about the house. She was having fun learning to sing the right way. Her voice was more forceful, but the thought of singing in front of thousands made her stomach churn.

With Morgan dreading the dentist's chair, she didn't tell him about the baby that night. After his root canals the next morning wasn't a good time to tell him, either. And she was no closer to an idea of how to break the news to him.

That night, Robert's phone call caught Morgan in the study. Callie was in the den reading.

"Hey, you're talking better," Robert said. "The wires came off all right?"

"They're off," Morgan said. "It wasn't easy going for me or for Callie. She fainted."

"Fainted? Odd. She was so strong during your hospital stay. And from her description, you looked inhuman."

"Well, this was a lot of pain. Not something I want to repeat." Morgan held the phone a moment while Robert repeated the conversation to Marilyn.

"Good news here. My agent sold Jeff's story to the Sunday supplement of the Johnson chain of newspapers. They're all over the country, so you'll get better coverage there than in any one single magazine."

"Great news. When will it be out?"

"The end of July. The lead time is usually longer, but the editor decided an article that he'd already scheduled didn't work. So, I imagine that picture of you and Jeff will be the cover. Just a second, Morgan."

He heard a muted conversation between Marilyn and Robert.

"Marilyn's concerned about Callie. She wants to know if Callie's been sick?"

"No. Well, she had a nervous stomach a couple of times when we were in the mountains, but that was because her father was coming over."

Again, Robert repeated the conversation to Marilyn.

"Was this sickness the first thing in the morning?" Robert asked.

"Yes. She woke up sick a couple of times. Once she emptied her stomach, she was okay. I've been worried about her. I think Phillip's presence in her life after all these years has really affected her. I know something's bothering her, and if it's not that, I don't know what it is." Morgan held on again and listened to a female squeal at Robert's end.

"Morgan, are you putting us on? Is this a secret?" Robert asked with a chuckle.

"Let me in on the joke," Morgan said.

"You really don't know?"

"Know what?"

"Put these words together and see what conclusion you draw. Callie's upset, morning sickness, fainting spell."

Morgan didn't reply. His mind reeled. Was Callie pregnant? Surely not. As much as they wanted a family, he'd told her how afraid he was for her to have a baby. What if it was stillborn like four of Grandma's babies? What if Callie died in childbirth like her mother?

"Morgan? Are you still there? Morgan?"

"I've got to go," Morgan said in a stunned voice and hung up the phone without saying goodbye.

His mind flashed back to Callie, sick in the mornings, eating crackers in bed. She'd cried when Jean was offered the teaching job. At the time he thought she was being a little emotional, but again he'd chalked it up to her new relationship with her dad. The secret, faraway look on her face that she wouldn't explain. Everything came back to him in a flood. Why hadn't he seen the obvious?

And why hadn't she told him? Did she think he'd be upset? Actually, he didn't know what he felt. He wanted to be a father, but his first concern was for Callie. Had she been to the doctor? If not, she was going right now, even if he had to cart her to the emergency room. If she had to lie in bed for nine months or seven months, or however long it took, he'd be at her side the entire time. He wondered when the baby was due. He needed some answers, now.

sixteen

Morgan bowed his head.

"God, I don't know how to ask her. She's the most important person in my world, and I'm afraid to ask her. What if I'm wrong? How will that make her feel? What do I say? Please guide me."

With a resolute squaring of his shoulders, he walked into the den. Callie sat with her head resting on the back of the rocking chair and her eyes closed. An open book lay in her lap.

Morgan sank to his knees in front of her. He closed the book and laid it on the floor, then took her hands in his.

She opened her eyes and sat up straight. For a long moment they stared at each other, both with unanswered questions, then Morgan placed a hand on Callie's stomach. Quick tears formed in Callie's eyes and rolled down her cheeks.

"We're going to have a baby, Morgan. I want you to be happy about it."

With a purposeful move, Morgan lifted her out of the chair and sat down, holding her.

"Now, Callie," he crooned. "Are you all right? Why didn't you tell me earlier? And when?"

"How did you know?" she said and sniffed, then added, "December."

"December. A Christmas baby. Have you been to the doctor?"

"Yes. I'm healthy and I'm taking my vitamins. I even

went Friday after I fainted, but I'm fine. And the baby's heart is as strong as ever."

"You've heard it?"

"Yes," she said and smiled. The same faraway look he'd seen before came in her eyes.

"Callie, I'm scared for you."

She turned in his arms and kissed him. "You have no reason to be scared. I'm healthy, I'm the perfect age for having a baby, and I want this baby so much."

"But Grandma . . . ."

"Grandma's babies were stillborn almost fifty years ago. Great medical strides have taken place since then. Don't you worry. This baby is going to be healthy and happy and loved."

Morgan rocked back and forth, holding her close to his heart. "Why didn't you tell me?"

"At first, I didn't want to tell you until I knew for sure. My doctor's appointment was on the Monday after your accident. I found out then, but I couldn't tell you. You couldn't talk, you were in pain. I thought you should concentrate on getting well and not worry about me." Callie took a deep breath. "I knew you had reservations about me being pregnant, and I didn't know how you'd feel about it. I didn't get pregnant on purpose. I wouldn't have consciously made that decision without you feeling the same way."

Morgan kissed the top of her head and continued rocking. "You know I'd like a houseful of children. But I want you more. I didn't want you taking risks with your health."

"But I'm not, Morgan. Come with me to the doctor next time, and you can talk to him. Oh, you can hear his heartbeat, too."

"His heartbeat?"

"I call the baby a him, but I don't know. What would you like?"

"A girl just as beautiful and kind as her mother."

Callie leaned away from his chest so she could look in his eyes. "I've kept this secret, but I thought I was doing the right thing. I didn't think you could handle it along with your injuries. You seemed so distant from me sometimes—like you were suffering alone. And I was here for you."

"Oh, Callie. I didn't want to burden you with how scared I was. It didn't seem manly, and it seemed pretty vain. It wasn't the pain so much as the emotional aspect. What would I look like? Would the fans accept me? Would I sing again? There were so many questions. And right there on top was why did God do this to me?"

"But He didn't."

"I know. We make choices . . . free will. But He's with me, and He's healing me, from the inside out. I've been out of control. I need to feel I'm controlling myself. I know I can't control others."

"I think we ultimately must turn over control of our lives to God. Master control. If we let Him influence our decisions and choices, then we can't go wrong, can we? Not really, anyway." She wiggled in his lap. "You want some chocolate?"

"Chocolate?"

"It's the one thing I'm crazy for. The best ones are those chocolate kisses with the nuts."

"And I thought you were crazy for me," Morgan said.

Callie laughed. "I am. If you were chocolate, I'd eat you up."

She started to get up, but Morgan held her firmly. "One more thing, Callie. We can't keep secrets from each other ever again. I couldn't explain your preoccupation, and I thought you were drifting away from me. You had good reasons for not telling me, but they were unfounded. Of course I worry about you, but I could have taken it and been as excited about the prospect of becoming a father as I am now. No more secrets?"

"No more secrets," she agreed.

He kissed her and she kissed him back with all the love they shared between them.

"Now I'm getting some chocolate."

The phone rang and Morgan answered while Callie put chocolate kisses in a bowl and brought them to the den.

"Were we right?" Robert asked without saying hello.

"Yes. Callie and I are having a baby in December."

"Congratulations, old man. You'll make a great dad, but you have to remember some of the scraps we got into and not be too hard on the little fellow."

Morgan laughed. "Just a minute," he said into the receiver. He explained the earlier phone conversation to Callie. "Should we ask them to be the godparents?"

"I can't think of anyone I'd rather have." Marilyn had helped her through a rough time last summer and had helped plan Morgan's concert for her church. Robert had been Morgan's best friend forever, well, until Callie had come on the scene. Callie smiled and repeated, "I can't think of anyone I'd rather have."

Morgan asked and waited until Robert conveyed the request to Marilyn. "They'd be honored," Morgan told Callie. "Marilyn wants to talk to you."

Callie took the phone and explained why she'd kept the news a secret. When she hung up, she turned to Morgan. "We need to tell your mother."

"What about Grandma?"

"She knows. She guessed almost before I knew. If we'd been around your mother more, I'm sure she'd have known, too. Mothers seem to have this intuitive instinct about other pregnant women."

Morgan phoned his mom and Victoria, then Callie called Grandma and explained that Morgan knew.

❧

The next morning Callie told Wilda and experienced the pleasure of being able to talk about the changes that were taking place physically within her.

"A baby," Jeff said, when Callie called him. "You should name him Jeff."

"I'll give it some thought," Callie said, "but remember that Morgan is the third. He might want a fourth, and let the tradition live on. Of course, it could be a girl."

"How about Jeffaleen? Jeffilou? Jeffereena?"

Callie laughed. "I'll mention your suggestions to Morgan." She called her father, and she called Jean. She told Harry when he phoned.

"Congratulations, Callie," he said, then switched the conversation to the concert. "We've set the date for August fifteenth in Yankee Stadium. How's Morgan doing with the voice lessons?"

"He's not there yet. Another week and the chord should be completely connected. He's still hoarse." Callie twisted the phone cord around her finger. "I'm taking lessons with him for the duet. I didn't think he'd make me do that." She had thought of asking Harry to talk him out of it, but then she remembered their new understanding not to keep their feelings from each other.

When Morgan came home from the office, and they were on their exercise walk around the grounds, she brought up the subject.

"Why do you want me to sing a duet with you? I'm no singer."

Morgan stopped walking and faced her. "On the day I mentioned it, my face had been cut to shreds, and I was striking out at anything. I didn't think you'd agree, and that would give me the perfect way out of doing a concert. Then after a while I thought that voice lessons, having to sing in front of me and a voice coach, might wear down your resistance to talking to me about what was bothering you."

"Then your reasons are no longer valid," Callie said.

"No. But I like singing with you. You have a good voice and we harmonize well, even with my croaky voice. But you don't have to go through with it. It's your decision."

"But you've written a song for us."

"True. But I can get backup singers to take your part. It's up to you, Callie. I should never have put you on the spot. I'm sorry."

She didn't know if she could do it. She prayed about it, and she continued with the lessons, practicing her part when she was alone. During the next few weeks, Morgan didn't press her about it, even when his hoarseness disappeared.

Finally the vocal chord had attached completely, and his voice was his own again. He thanked God that his ordeal was over at last. Callie was jubilant with Morgan's complete physical recovery, but as the time neared for the concert, she still hadn't made a decision about singing with him. Did he really need her on stage now that he knew he could sing again?

&

Callie and Morgan left for New York two days ahead of the scheduled concert. Morgan's new front teeth couldn't be distinguished from his own. His chin held only a small scar that Callie told him gave him character.

Grandma had agreed to come with Dorothy and Victoria's family. Jeff had conned tickets out of Morgan, and he was flying in with the others. "I won't be a burden," he'd said. "I can walk alone okay."

He was still a little unstable on his feet, although he'd graduated from the walker to crutches by the middle of July and had been walking alone now for over a week. By getting in the stadium early with Morgan and the others, he wouldn't be subjected to the jarring crowds of a couple of hours later.

Robert's article on Jeff and Morgan and their struggle to overcome their accidents came out three weeks before the concert date. Letters against drunk drivers had poured into the newspaper offices, and loyalty to Morgan had precipitated a sold-out concert.

The day before the performance, Callie went with Morgan to Yankee Stadium to look at the stage that had been erected. Sound equipment was being connected, and Morgan sang a few songs, without one crack in his voice and absolutely no hoarseness. When he started on the duet, even without the backup singers, Callie joined in.

She didn't know if she could sing it with him the next night, and he had told her she could decide at the last minute. Stage fright could paralyze her; he knew because he suffered from it. Less now than in the past, and knowing how close he'd come to never performing again, he'd come to grips with it. He didn't want to give up singing. If his career required a concert a year, filmed for TV viewing later, he'd do it.

On the day of the concert, Morgan and Callie stayed in the hotel until after the others had arrived late that morning. This was Grandma's first trip to New York, and she was all eyes and open mouth at the sights as a limo carried them around Manhattan. Robert and Marilyn invited everyone to their apartment for lunch and after another hour of sightseeing for Grandma, the group relaxed in the hotel.

At three-thirty they left for the stadium for the eight o'clock show. Touring the stadium, eating in the restaurant, and watching final preparations for the performance filled the hours until show time.

"This is different than the concert we arranged for Morgan last summer," Marilyn said. The fallow land of a church member had been used for parking, and the audience had sat on lawn chairs and blankets. Two flatbed trucks had served as the stage.

"But the same excitement is here," Callie said. The group sat in the dressing room, waiting for the big moment as fans noisily filled the stadium.

Morgan had decided against a warm-up group. This was his come-back concert, and it would be his alone. He'd give the fans two hours of songs. "If you want to sing," he told Callie, moments before walking onto the field, "be ready by nine-thirty. It's the next to last song."

Callie nodded. Morgan always closed with "Amazing Grace." He'd use the spot before it to plug his new song. It hadn't been recorded as a single yet, but that was scheduled for back in the studio next week. Unless, as Harry had said, it went so well tonight that it would be released as a live recording, complete with the response of the crowd.

At five minutes before eight, Morgan's band walked to the stage and tuned up their instruments. Morgan and Callie stood together in the tunnel that led to the field and asked God to bless the concert and to give Morgan courage to sing in public.

"Ladies and gentlemen," the announcer's voice came loud

and clear over the sound system. "In his first appearance since his accident last spring, please welcome Trey."

Morgan walked onto the field, cameras capturing his image on the brand new scoreboard. The fans roared and stood in an ovation for him before he'd sung a note. Morgan was so choked up at their support that a full five minutes passed before he started his first song, but the fans' cheers hadn't died down by then anyway.

He started with "Callie's Song" and interspersed some of his old hits with new songs he'd written. The only break he took was when the band played an instrumental.

When the time neared for the duet, it was Callie's turn to ask God for courage. She knew Morgan wanted her to sing with him, and she wanted to. She knew the words by heart. Now if she could only get them out in front of sixty thousand people.

When he started the song before the duet, she walked to the stage and sat on the steps, waiting for her cue. At least she could stand by him even if she couldn't get one word past the huge lump in her throat. She waited for the audience's applause that signaled the end of the song, then she climbed the stairs and walked to Morgan's side.

He didn't have to explain who Callie was when she joined him. The crowd knew. He put his arm around her and drew her toward the mike. In a wifely gesture, Callie reached up and brushed back the hair that had fallen on his forehead. She looked into his eyes, saw his love, and knew she could sing for him.

"Callie and I are proud to share our joy with you," he announced, and his arm tightened around her. "We're having a baby in December." It hadn't been in a press release, no rumors had leaked out, and the mood of the crowd was that these dear friends had just shared a secret with them, all sixty thousand of them.

When the crowd noise died down, the band began on the duet. Callie took a deep breath, then sang in a clear sweet voice:

> "Our lives are joined with love's promise,
> Old as time, but still brand new."

Then Morgan sang,

> "With the joy of song and laughter,
> We come to share our lives with you."

Their voices combined in a rich harmony:

> "We walk, we run, we climb, we stumble
> Through life's triumph and its woe.
> But through it all God gives a strength
> We wish that every heart could know."

When they finished the song, Morgan and Callie held hands and faced each other, as they had done when they had taken their wedding vows.

"You are wonderful," Morgan whispered.

"I love you," Callie whispered back.

The crowd erupted. Callie stayed on the stage while Morgan sang his traditional final song, then together they walked off the field.

"What are you going to do next year for an encore?" Harry said as they entered the dressing room. "Last year you asked her to marry you. This year you tell the fans you're having a baby. How can you top that?"

Morgan laughed. "We'll give it some thought," he said.

epilogue

"Push, Callie, push," Morgan urged. "I can see the head."

She'd been in the hospital only five hours, and he had expected a longer labor than this. He'd read everything he could find on natural delivery and had gone through classes with Callie. Now that the moment had come, he couldn't believe that he was actually witnessing the miracle of birth.

She squeezed his hand, stopping the circulation in his fingers, but he didn't care. She could have cut off his hand if that would have made this easier for her. Morgan wiped the perspiration from her forehead.

"All right, push again," the doctor said in a calm voice. "This is it."

Callie grunted as she gave a final push.

"It's a girl," the doctor announced.

Callie exhaled as relief flooded through her. She glanced at Morgan, whose eyes were shining with joy.

"It's a girl," she echoed the doctor's words. "Is that okay?"

"It's perfect." Morgan took the baby from the nurse, who had quickly wiped her off and wrapped her in a pink blanket. He laid the baby next to Callie, and kissed first his wife and then his child, all the while giving thanks to God that they were both all right.

"Do you have a name picked out?" the nurse asked.

"No," Callie said.

"Yes," Morgan answered at the same time.

"We do?"

"I'd like to name her Daisy," he said.

"You want to name her after my mother?"

"Without Daisy, I wouldn't have you. I owe her more than a namesake."

Tears streamed down Callie's face. "Hi, Daisy," she whispered to the child. "I love you."

A Letter To Our Readers

Dear Reader:

In order that we might better contribute to your reading enjoyment, we would appreciate your taking a few minutes to respond to the following questions. When completed, please return to the following:

Rebecca Germany, Editor
Heartsong Presents
P.O. Box 719
Uhrichsville, Ohio 44683

1. Did you enjoy reading *Callie's Challenge*?
   ❑ Very much. I would like to see more books
      by this author!
   ❑ Moderately
      I would have enjoyed it more if _____

   _____

2. Are you a member of **Heartsong Presents**? ❑Yes ❑No
   If no, where did you purchase this book?_____

   _____

3. What influenced your decision to purchase this
   book? (Check those that apply.)

   ❑ Cover   ❑ Back cover copy

   ❑ Title   ❑ Friends

   ❑ Publicity   ❑ Other_____

4. How would you rate, on a scale from 1 (poor) to 5
   (superior), **Heartsong Presents'** new cover design?_____

5. On a scale from 1 (poor) to 10 (superior), please rate the following elements.

___Heroine   ___Plot

___Hero   ___Inspirational theme

___Setting   ___Secondary characters

6. What settings would you like to see covered in **Heartsong Presents** books?_____

_____

_____

7. What are some inspirational themes you would like to see treated in future books?_____

_____

_____

8. Would you be interested in reading other **Heartsong Presents** titles?   ❏ Yes   ❏ No

9. Please check your age range:
   ❏ Under 18   ❏ 18-24   ❏ 25-34
   ❏ 35-45   ❏ 46-55   ❏ Over 55

10. How many hours per week do you read? _____

Name _____

Occupation _____

Address _____

City_____ State_____ Zip _____

Veda Boyd Jones

___*Gentle Persuasion*—Dallas Stone, former major league pitcher, represents everything Julie Russell despises, yet she is strangely drawn to him. Can gentle persuasion help both Julie and Dallas find room for each other's gifts? HP21 $2.95

___*Under a Texas Sky*—Abby Kane is caught in a stampede of emotions when her hometown is selected as the location for an upcoming movie. Called in to assist screenwriter Rob Vincent, Abby is soon captivated by both the process of making movies and the man himself. HP34 $2.95

___*The Governor's Daughter*—Landon shares Gayle's faith in God and her fascination with politics, but Gayle resists his attempts to discover her true identity. Hurt once already, she has no desire to be loved only as the governor's daughter. HP46 $2.95

___*A Sign of Love*—Andrea Cooper is comfortable with her life as a high school history teacher, president of the local historical preservation society, and active church member. Comfortable, that is, until Grant Logan bursts into her life. HP78 $2.95

___*Callie's Mountain*—"Summer folk and year-rounders don't mix." Yet, Callie can't help having a dream of love with her one-time benefactor Morgan Rutherford. But who is Morgan...the handsome Christian gentleman or the brazen country crooner? HP110 $2.95

········· Presents ·········

Great Inspirational Romance at a Great Price!

Heartsong Presents books are inspirational romances in contemporary and historical settings, designed to give you an enjoyable, spirit-lifting reading experience. You can choose from 156 wonderfully written titles from some of today's best authors like Colleen L. Reece, Brenda Bancroft, Janelle Jamison, and many others

When ordering quantities less than twelve, above titles are $2.95 each.